UNDERWORLD FORTUNE ENTERTAINMENT
PRESENTS

BEDROOM THUG

MAY 10, 2019
LULU PRESS
Underworld Fortune Entertainment

©2019

ISBN-13: 978-0-9905736-0-9

Sexual liberation implies the liberation of the Whole being:

Mind, Body, and Spirit. This holistic viewpoint is an essential ingredient to the understanding of the sexual secrets.

-Nik Douglas

DEDICATION

Sometimes a journey can begin without your knowledge. It may come to you disguised as an artistic spark of imagination, or it may be lit by the fuse of a muse unspoken. I've been fortunate in my travels, encountering many people who have come in to my life and helped me spark, igniting the fire that has enlightened my path. As my work stretches into thousands of words, there are many people who must be thanked. To my brother K-Born, and his beautiful wife queen Naqueeba Earth, for having my back and believing in my talent. Your support and affection have kept my light burning in the belly of the beast. I want to thank my lovely, beautiful wife Nya-B, whose love and devotion kept me warm through the coldest times. Without your support and patience I would never have been able to live my dreams. I appreciate her reading of every word of this book over and over. She largely made my work possible. To all my kids who opened my eyes globally to how life is so precious, daddy will always have y'all backs. To their mothers, thanks for turning your backs when life happened. I'm not mad because your abandonment motivated me more to work harder and my focus got sharper through the mist of battles. To my wonderful mother, you will always be missed, and I know you're so proud of the man I've become. To my sisters, love conquers all. Aunt Nanette, you the best and thanks for always being there for me and my sisters. To the Jackie Brown, you're a good-hearted person and I thank you for your incredible diligence in helping me with this endeavor. To my Cousin Shanda Florida, one of the most determined person I know. Go check her out on Facebook[t-apparel/1616].

Last, but far from the least, my strong likeminded and independent thinking comrades at constant war on the streets and in the belly of the beast; Nitty Bangs, D-Box, J-30, Frank-White, Hook Off, Pop-a-Lot, Pop-Off, Grim, R.L, G.L, Rampage, Hell Rell, 40, Big Dogz, Dizzy, Lou-Diamonds, Lex-Diamonds, Craz-o, H.P, Snoop, Fame, I-Shine, Butter, Ill Kid, Soul-

B, Double-R, Bugsy, Gotti, Face, Dogz, Hollywood, Sonny-Blanca, Braveheart, Polo, Pretty-Sha, Crime, Glock, Bear, Bronxtail, Hova, Boom, Tyson, B-Boy, Big-b, Poe, Hot-Boy, Blackseed, Blackheart, Peewee, Brim, Bad Vibe, Dick Wolf, Cross Brim, Larry-O, Robo just[R.I.P], Big dog, Ant Live, Live-Wire, Jux, Comrade, Tommy Guns, Ra-Guns, Loons, Spooky, Mel-Murda, Shane[R.I.P], Doe-Boy, Ghost, Styles, Boogie, Get-Low, Eli-Brim, Eco, B-Spot, blaze, Kev-Moe, G-Stacks, Un-Gambino, S.I,L.B, Hell Razor, B.G, Fats, Pimp Juice, Tank Head, Pistol Pete, Ty Guns, Ty-Ty[R.I.P], ra-Digga, Be-Moe, Water Bug, Murda Brim, Byson, Miky B, Bang-Bang, Main Brim, Bad Azz, Pretty Black, E-Scar, A.B, Y.G, B.O, D-Block, Red-Lite, P-Funk, fingers, S.O, O.G Dead Eye, O.G Mack, Scar, Bush, Bishop, Cream, blakko Mackko, Moe Shae, John Boy, WildChild, , Drama[R.I.P], Spice, Enfer-red, Scrapy, cheecks, Touch, Bos-Scooter, Hoe, Magoo, Ice-Berg, Smoke, Kev-Frost, Charlie-Rock, Mafia, Manifest, Life, True, War-God, A-Train, Himo, Mellow, Slike, Mazaraddi Fox[R.I.P],

Sherm-Da-Worm, MK, Bizz, Nard, Trap, and the whole underworld family…

On the first day out of prison, Dominique Vox, made it home without anyone aware of his homecoming. He wanted it that way He was ashamed of his run-ins with the law. Dominque felt that he had put a blemish on the family name with his appetite for fast, easy money. He still carried that shame on the day of his release, after doing 11 years in prison. When exiting the train station in his old neighborhood, he made it his duty not to encounter anyone. He really wasn't ready to deal with the looks, whispers, and judgement due to a lifestyle that he had put behind him so long ago. Dominique lived in the Clinton Hills section of Brooklyn, New York. In his neighborhood people grinded daily to afford their brownstone houses and nice cars. Living a life of crime was not an option. Working hard to earn paycheck after paycheck with the anticipation of a raise or bonus in the same year, was the only way. He knew how the people in his neighborhood felt about criminals, which was one of the main reasons he chose to keep a low profile.

Dominique jumped in the shower to rinse away what he hoped was the last stint of prison. After rubbing coconut oil all over his body, he draped his toned chest with a white wife beater and slid on a pair of grey sweatpants that his bulge printed perfectly. Before heading to his mother's bedroom, he bumped in to his grandfather. The conversation lasted for what seemed to be hours. Dominique finally made his way to his mother's room inhaling deeply hoping to smell just an inkling of his mother's essence. He glanced around the room trying not to let the guilt and sadness of her absence consume him. Dominique began pulling out shoe box after shoe box full of pictures of his mother, Ms. Elayne, from her happier days. Each box was empty. Soon, every photo his mother owned was scattered all over the bed. With each picture the pain in his heart swelled. He truly felt that the added stress he brought on his mother, added to her illness. Ms. Elayne died of breast cancer four years into his prison sentence. The pain consumed so much of Dominique's energy he could no longer hold back his tears. He had never really allowed his self to grieve her. He could not allow his emotions to show behind bars. It would make him a target. The tears escaped his eyes forcefully without any restraint. Drained Dominique fell into a deep slumber across his mother's bed. He woke up two o'clock in the morning and started to clean the kitchen. It was a task he dreaded in his younger years, but now as a man, he realized it was just a simple task his mother would ask of him.

After the kitchen was spotless, Dominique grabbed two large garbage bags, and took them outside to the dumpster. As he was doing this, a white Audi RS5 pulled up, and parked in front of his neighbor's house next door. Before entering back into his house, a familiar sweet voice called his name with such style and grace, "DOMINIQUE!"

As he turned around, his eyes did a slow crawl over the full length of this incredible body standing in front of him. Her name was Rebecca. She was older than Dominique. She was wearing a black Saint Laurent dress, which complimented her curves. Her skin was flawless, the color of rich milk. She had real beauty the type that could make even the smoothest talker, stutter. This woman has always been gorgeous in his eyes. He lusted over her since he was younger, and Ms. Rebecca looked like she hadn't aged one bit. He gave her a charming smile, "How you doing Ms. Rebecca?"

Ms. Rebecca had a very successful catering

business that she started almost 20 years ago. Through her business she met and became very close friends with some of New York City elite. Anytime there was an exquisite function, she was the first to be called. She could cook anything for any occasion.

"I knew that was you. Come here and let me take a good look at you.", she cooed.

Dominique walked towards her like a male supermodel, all the while hoping that no one else would notice him. As soon as she was in arms reach, they embraced. She felt so small and soft in his arms. Her body fragrance was mixed with a hint of alcohol, but still was a sweet and intoxicating scent to him. Impressive, she thought to herself. She rubbed her hands up and down his chiseled back. She wanted so bad to squeeze his ass, but decided to keep it classy, at least for now. Finally, their arms detangled from each other and they began to talk.

"So, when did you get out?", she

questioned. He couldn't believe how freely she asked her question. It was if she asked if he was home from college.

"I got home today." he responded. "Last time I seen you was at Ms. Elayne's farewell. My, have you grown." She stated as she stared him over.

"Yeah, I know. That was over 7 years ago. I'm 30 years old now.", informed Dominique.

"Oh, is that so?", she flirted. Ms. Rebecca's flirting made Dominique blush.

"Yeah, that's so, Ms. Rebecca.", he flirted back.

"What are your plans?", she asked in a whispery type voice. Kind of flirtatious, however Dominique wasn't sure if she was flirting or if the alcohol had taken over. As she's spoke to him, her hands conveniently grazed his abs and chest.

"Just taking things one day at a time and trying to go that legal route for a change, why wassup?", he asked.

"Have you eaten a decent meal yet?", she asked.

"Actually, no. I haven't had a chance to do anything yet, really.".

"Good, come over by my place tomorrow, around six., so I can make you a decent meal. I know it's been a while since you had one.", stated Rebecca.

"You don't have to do that Ms. Rebecca, I know you're a very busy woman and have other things to do."

"Come on, I would love to, and besides, I'm not taking no for an answer.", she insisted. Her suggestion was more like an order rather than an offer. He was a little taken back by her persistence, however weirdly flattered about the offer.

"Well, since you insist, I guess I could swing by.", Dominique reluctantly accepted.

"Good then. We all set for tomorrow at six.", she stated as she winked her left eye and curved her lips into a sexy smirk. Dominique couldn't help but blush. Ms. Rebecca knew exactly what she was doing. Little did he know, it was only the beginning. She saw that he was speechless and shocked by her forwardness, so she decided to leave him with that, so he had something to dwell over later. Less is more, she thought to herself. She initiated another hug, but this time, it was more passionate. She tippy-toed and kissed him on his chest, releasing her embrace, and walked away as if nothing happened.

"Smooches", she said, as she walked away. She knew he was staring, so she put a little extra switch in her hips. Dominique never said a word or moved a single limb, but his eyes did. They bounced along the rhythm of her glorious rump. He was in deep lust. Rebecca lusted too. Thinking how good Dominique looked in his wife beater and sweatpants. Mr. Vox had grown into such a handsome man.

The following morning, Dominique was up and dressed by 8am. He was ready to start his day. He had a positive attitude and was ready for the first day of starting over. Job searching was his priority of the day. He started his job expedition in Manhattan and worked his way to downtown Brooklyn. He filled out applications for Foot Locker, The Barclays Center, and numerous other clothing stores. The jobs that interviewed him on the spot, was interested up until the moment he told them he had a criminal record. Their demeanor would change instantly, and he was no longer a candidate. He knew he didn't have a chance to be hired. Although he started the day being very optimistic, reality started to set in, and so did the disappointment. He didn't let it discourage him though. Tomorrow would be another day. He remembered his dinner plans that day with Ms. Rebecca. He decided to head home so he could prepare. Within an hour, Dominique was home, in the shower, washing away his sweat from the day events. After prepping for an hour, he headed over to Ms. Rebecca's house. When he got there, he rang the bell twice, and as he was about to ring the third time, the door opened. There stood Ms. Rebecca in a loosely closed white robe. The first thing he noticed was how the robe hugged her body to perfection. His gaze lingered to her breast, which was spilling out through the open part of the robe. Ms. Rebecca was a voluptuous woman. A thrill swept through his body. He fought the urge to open the top of her robe even more. Ms. Rebecca enjoyed the way Dominique stared at her. For her to get that type of reaction from such a younger man, was very empowering. She felt desirable and sexy.

"Are you going to just stand there and stare at me or your planning on coming inside?", she asked. Dominique didn't say a word. He just stepped inside and walked right up to her and kissed her on the cheek. He did that to let her subconsciously know that he was not intimidated by her beauty. The setting inside of Ms. Rebecca's house was very romantic. She had the lights dimmed with jazz music playing in the background by Dexter Gorden. Ms. Rebecca loved her some Dexter Gorden, a saxophonist that had the gift to put her body in a trance. As far as she was concerned Dexter always set the mood.

"Is that the legendary Dexter Gorden playing?", Dominique asked.

"Why yes, that is, he's the best.", replied Rebecca.

"That would be an understatement. He's more like the greatest jazz saxophonist who ever lived. God bless his soul.", responded Dominique.

Ms. Rebecca was very impressed with his knowledge of her favorite musician. Typically guys his age was into rap music. He scored some major points for this one. It was good to know he wasn't just all body. What other knowledge did he possess, she wondered. She escorted Dominique to her dining room area. The dining table had two long lit candles, burning vanilla aroma into the air. The aroma was calming to Dominique's nose. He liked it. As soon as he sat down, she walked away to get their plate of food. He was watching as the fabric of her robe was inching upwards, wedging tightly between her ass, exposing the luscious curves of her butt. Dominique was thoroughly aroused. He had sex before he got locked up, with this one girl. Even though they had sex multiple times, they still didn't have enough experience to know what they were doing. They were each other's first. Ms. Rebecca had Dominique so turned on that his dick was tenting up his boxer shorts with pre-cum something fierce. The rumbling in the kitchen snapped him out of his private thoughts.

"Do you need some help in there, Ms. Rebecca?", Dominque asked.

"No, I have everything under control, you just relax.", she assured him.

Dominique decided to pour himself a glass of red wine, sat back and begin enjoying the soothing sound of jazz music. While sitting at the dining room table waiting on Ms. Rebecca, Dominique begin looking at the scenery of her style and taste. The living room décor was antiques but elegant. Dominique loved how the white, gold and mirrors complimented each other. The painting on the wall enhanced the whole inside of the house all together. One grabbed his attention and held it longer than the rest. It was an oil painting of Ms. Rebecca, lying seductively across a baby grand piano in the nude. Dominique thought the painting was beautiful of course, but it didn't capture her full beauty.

"Ms. Rebecca, you have a very beautiful

place!", exclaimed Dominique.

"Thank you. A very dear friend of mine decorated it. According to Architectural Digest. She's the best in the city. I could have sworn you been in my house before.".

"No, this is my first time. I'm sure of it.", he replied.

"Well then, I will have to show you the rest of the house later."

"I'd love that!", he replied with a smile.

Seconds later, Ms. Rebecca came out of the kitchen carrying both of their plates. She placed one on her side of the table and one in front of Dominique, giving him a better view of her cleavage. This time she caught him staring at them, like two precious gems.

"Don't it look delicious?", she asked with a smirk.

"Yessss very delicious.", answered Dominique, looking a little embarrassed that she had caught him staring at her breast. Ms. Rebecca started to laugh, "I meant the food, honey.".

"Oh, I'm sorry.", said Dominique as he snapped out his trance.

"Sorry for what? Eyes fixate on what they like", she replied.

In an attempt to change the direction of the conversation, Dominique interrupted, "It looks delicious, what is it?".

"It's smoked salmon with citrus salsa, brown rice cooked in bone broth, broccoli and tomatoes.", described Ms. Rebecca.

"It sounds even more delicious than it looks.", he complimented.

The aroma alone made his mouth salivate. Ms. Rebecca walked to her side of the table and sat down to get ready to eat her favorite meal. Dominique had a pleasing look on his face but underneath he was saying to himself how was he supposed to get full from these small portions. He was used to eating hearty meals. In his eyes, the plate looks like a kid's meal.

"So, how was your day?", asked Ms.

Rebecca.

"Filled out a couple applications, even scored some on the spot interviews, however it doesn't look promising.", Dominique answered with the slight sound of defeat in his tone.

"Don't let it hinder you, something is going to fall through.", he said with a wink.

"Yeah, I know. I just hope it fall through soon.".

"Just keep applying yourself.", she encouraged.

After an hour of eating and conversing, Dominique began feeling the wine. Ms. Rebecca was as well. She had the bottle for a few years, she was holding it for a special occasion and this occasion was very much special, as far as Ms. Rebecca was concerned.

"So, would you like to see the rest of the house?", she asked.

"Ok, sure.", he replied.

They both got up from the table. She was leading the way and Dominique was following, enjoying the view. Ms. Rebecca showed him every room of the house but left her bedroom for the "grand finale".

"Last, but not least, the Queen's Lair.", she laughed as she opened the door. She stepped inside with him still close behind. Dominique was not surprised at how decadent and desirable her bedroom looked. The fire place in the far corner of her room made the exhibit dreamier. Ms. Rebecca turned around to see if Dominique enjoyed the tour of her house. He was directly in front of her, staring into her big blue eyes.

"So, what do you think?" she asked.

He replied by drawing her closer to him and kissing her on the lips. Although, caught off guard, Ms. Rebecca kissed him back. Her lips were really soft against his. He began to kiss her neck, while opening her robe, exposing her naked body. The site of her nakedness made Dominique aroused all over again, as he was in the dining room.

The sensation of his kisses instantly made her wet between the legs. She slipped her right hand into his pants. A little taken back by how well-endowed he was, but heavily turned on. She takes it out his boxers. She was not aware of his inexperience with sex. She just knew that she liked what she felt and wanted more. As she was stroking his long succulent cock, she slowly dropped to her knees in front of him. She licks the pre-cum from the tip of his dick, before she fully mounts him. Her dick sucking skills was driving him insane. The feeling was welcoming, but unbearable at the same time. It drained energy from his legs. He pulls his dick out of her mouth and makes her stand up. He turns her around and bends her over the side of the bed, spreads her legs apart and begins to finger fuck her from the back. First, he roughly inserts one finger, then two, then three...as her moans got louder, the harder he inserted. As he felt her cream on his fingers, he removed his fingers and made her get back on her knees to suck him off some more. She was loving the way he took control. As she licked up and down the shaft of his dick, he began to moan lightly. The sounds he made had her ready for whatever pain and pleasure was to come next. He didn't want to cum just yet, so he pulled his dick from her mouth again. This time, she gets up and walks over towards the bed. She signals him seductively with one finger for him to come over. As he walks over, he is removing his remaining clothing from his body. She laid across the bed, on her back and spread her legs, prepared for whatever action Dominique wanted to bring. It could be oral or anal. At this point, it didn't matter. She just needed to get off again. He sized up the situation, then reached over and parted her legs a little further, giving him some room to operate. He carefully aimed and when he found his target, he started to pound her with his cock. Each stroke had a massive impact. Ms. Rebecca was loving every minute of it. When she came, she came HARD. He came seconds after. They went another round and finally both collapsed from exhaustion. She curled up next to him, laying her head on his broad shoulders and chest, trying to catch her breath.

"My God, that was wonderful!", she looked up at him to see if he agreed. The look on his face let her know he was more than satisfied. They both were relaxed and enjoying the sound of each other's heavy breathing. After thoroughly assessing Dominique's talents Rebecca thought that it would be the perfect time to present him with a proposition.

"You know, you could make some good money off that tool you're carrying.", she said with a quick wink and a smile. Dominique was blushing from the nice compliment.

"No, seriously.", she continued, now with a more serious look on her face.

"Dominique this is a lucrative opportunity. You have all the qualities necessary to make a lot of money. Your handsome. Have a gorgeous body. Intelligent. Charming.

Most of all, you're a fantastic fuck. I'm just saying. You could make some good money.".

"I know I need a job, Ms. Rebecca, but don't you think that's a little farfetched?", Dominique asked, looking perplexed.

"First off, you can call me Rebecca. No need for the formal after what we just did. Secondly, it's not farfetched. It's a great idea and excellent opportunity. Lastly, you wouldn't need a job, because you would be your own boss. As a matter of fact, we could be business partners. I'm more suited to make it work. I have the resources and the intellect to make sure every angle is covered.".

It was in that moment that Dominique realized that she was more than serious. She was very adamant at this point.

"With all due respect, Rebecca, you got to be out of your fucking mind. I was just released from prison yesterday, and I'm trying to get my life together. Before leaving prison, I promised myself to make some serious life changes. I gave up that criminal lifestyle and what you're talking about sounds illegal as fuck.".

"Look, we as human beings have essential qualities, Dominique, that makes us special and worthy. Yours just happens to be that great big dick. Which is a perfect accessory, I might add. You should be thankful that the good lord blessed you with a bigger than average sized dick and adequate knowledge of how to use it. There aren't many who have been blessed with both my dear. What I'm presenting to you is a lucrative business opportunity. You will never have to come into contact with the law. My associates would rather keep their meetings with you very quiet....and again, look at it as a business opportunity. You're not going to be walking the sidewalk like some low-end prostitute. More like a professional escort. High end. High quality. Boss business.", she said with a determined smile. Dominique couldn't believe he was having this conversation and WHO he was having this conversation with. This is the same lady he lusted after for 20 years. Never in his wildest dreams could he have seen himself laying up with her.... let alone discussing her pimping him out. He was still exhausted after releasing eleven years of pinned up prison stress. Eleven whole years of no intimacy. Nothing whatsoever. Not even the simplest thing, like a scent of a woman. Shit, he hadn't even smelled a flower in the past eleven years. He didn't want to spoil the moment by continuing to disagree with her extreme idea of him selling sex. He was flattered, because the only experience he had sexually was before he got locked up at 19 years old. That one girl. So, yes, he was extremely flattered by Ms. Rebecca's talk about his "elevated skills". She was very persistent and demanded that he at least consider it.

"OK, I'm not saying yes, but I'm not saying no at this time. I am saying, I will think about it.", Dominique reluctantly agreed.

"Fair enough", Ms. Rebecca replied. After a couple more minutes of random conversation, her voice lowered into a whisper, and then she nodded off into a comatose like slumber. She held onto him, like he was her new teddy bear and she was a toddler. Dominique closed his eyes and reviewing the day events till he fell asleep.

Weeks passed with no luck of finding a job. Dominique went to a temp agency that specialized in employing parolees. The agency got him a few odd jobs, most of them he didn't like. Still, he dealt with it because he knew something greater was soon coming. Several weeks later, it did. A permanent position at a restaurant in Manhattan as a cook.

Dominique loved his job. He loved cooking more. That was the only reason he dealt with his manager's unprofessional ways. Cooking was something his mother taught him at a young age. His mother told him to never rely on a woman to take care of him. Most of what his mother told him when he was young, helped him in the streets and throughout his prison sentence. Everybody at the restaurant knew he was an ex-felon because of his manager, Rob. Rob didn't like Dominique. He thought Dominique was a con man that had everyone else fooled with his charming ways. The real reason he didn't like Dominique was because his father, Mr. Mike, who took a strong liking to Dominique. As a result, Rob would try to provoke Dominique. Dominique was aware of Rob's true intentions, so he did everything he could to avoid Rob. He completed his duties for eight hours and went home. At the end of his shift he was always way more tired than the rest of the staff. Rob had him doing his job, and additional tasks, things that were not even part of his job description. Some of his co-workers also grew animosity toward him for no other reason than to appease Rob. There was one of his co-workers that stuck out from the rest, she spoke to him. Most of the time went out of her way just to do so. Dominique found her to be very beautiful. He loved her dark, almond shaped eyes, but kept it strictly professional. After weeks of working at the restaurant, Dominique walked into work on time, as he normally done, but this particular day was kind of different. All his co-workers were sitting in the spacious dining room area listening to Rob announcing some money being missing. Dominique knew there was something wrong because soon as he walked in, everyone was giving him bitter stares.

"Right on time, Mr. Vox.", said Rob, with a hint of sarcasm.

"I'm always on time. Not one time have I come in here late.", Dominique proclaimed.

"Well that don't matter anymore.", ranted Rob.

"What do you mean?", asked Dominique.

"I don't know any other way to put this, so I'm just going to keep it short and sweet. Some money came up missing and you're the only one here with a criminal background. I'm sorry to say this Dom, but your services are no longer needed here!".

Dominique began staring at him filled with contempt, trying to hold his temper back.

"Are you accusing me of stealing, Rob? Why would I want to steal from here? You trying to set me up?", Dominique snarled.

"Just be lucky we've decided not to involve police in the matter.", said Rob.

Dominique turned around and walked out of the restaurant without saying another word, with fire burning in his stomach. He wanted to hurt Rob so bad, but prison kept popping up in the forefront of his head, so he declined the thought by just walking out. After about an hour or so, he arrived home, and went straight to his bedroom. He laid across the bed in the dark, contemplating his next move. Three hours later, the sound of his house phone ringing, woke him up out of his sleep. He saw that it was Ms. Rebecca's number on the caller I.D., so he picked it up.

"Hello.", said Dominique in a sleepy and

somber voice.

"Hey, how you been doing stranger?", asked Ms. Rebecca. She could sense something was wrong.

"To be truthful, not too good.", said Dominique.

"I can tell… Do you want to talk about it?", asked Ms. Rebecca.

"I got fired today.", Dominique stated.

"I'm so sorry to hear that.", replied Rebecca.

"It's a minor setback. I'll find another job."

"Look Dominique, have you given any thought to what we discussed?"

"Well, when I had a job, I really didn't need to." he replied.

"Well… you don't now and…"., she continued. He cut her off mid-sentence,

"Look, I'm too stressed out right now to be having this conversation with you.", He stated, a little annoyed with the subject.

"Okay.", she replied, "You should stop by...maybe I can help you relieve some of your stress."

He knew exactly what she was insinuating. It had been weeks since their last encounter. Finally, something he did agree with her on. He needed some sexual healing.

"Hello, are you still there?", she asked, interrupting his train of thought.

"Yeah, I'm still here." He replied.

"Give me about an hour." He continued.

They both agreed and hung up. Before he left his house, he received a text message from Rebecca, informing him that she will be leaving her front door unlocked. As soon as he arrived at the house, and opened the door, he found that the scenery was warm and relaxing with rose petals leading to the bathroom. He closed the door and proceeded to go towards the bathroom area.

When he opened the door, he was please to find Rebecca soaking in a milk bath. The milk soaked her hair, ran down her face and across her full breast. Her skin was glistening. Neither of them spoke a word to each other. There was no need. They both knew what was expected. He got undressed and stepped in the oval tub beside Rebecca. The temperature of the water was just right. It was very warm and liberating. Rebecca proceeding to climb on top of him in a straddling position and tightened her thighs around him. She began gently stroking his head and caressing the muscles in his neck to release the tension in it. Dominique trembled a little because the sensation sent a shock wave through his body. He had his eyes closed, allowing the sensation to last a little longer as it ran from his head to his toes. Rebecca kissed Dominique very deeply and seductively. He kissed her back. As he began to nibble on her neck, she gently grabbed his dick and slid it inside of her. Straddling him, he gently grabs the back of her head by her hair and pulls her back and started to work his kisses down to her desirable breast. His lips sent waves of excitement up her spine as she gently rode

him. As he flicked his tongue over her hardening nipples, she began to increase the strength of her thrust on his dick.
Dominique penetrated her deeply as her pussy muscles squeezed tightly around him. He loved every moment. Especially the sensation of her pussy walls hugging him. Her rhythm and thrust increased.
Dominique began to move in and out in sync with the rhythm of her body. She came down to meet him on every deep thrust, until she finally creamed on him and he came inside of her. He stayed inside her. She exhausted herself to the point that she just collapsed on his chest. She could hear the pounding of his heart beat. He hugged her.

"I feel so alive when I'm with you.", She said. He hugged her tighter and kissed her forehead.

"So, Dominique, are you going to give me an answer to my business proposition?".

Dominique sat in silence momentarily, letting the question bounce around in his head. He was experiencing internal conflict. Possible financial gain? Self-destruction? A voice kept murmuring in his head, telling him not to do it. A familiar voice. A voice with sincere intentions. It was his mother's voice. He knew his mother would be disappointed in him if he did it. He felt that his mother would be hurt knowing that he would be doing it for money and not for true love. Then the thought of needing and wanting to survive took over. He could get this money, stack it, and as soon as he makes enough, he would just walk away. What was the harm, really? Getting paid to do what most men like to do; FUCK and n receive gifts and money in exchange for it. They get off, and so does he. It sounded like a win-win situation. What could possibly go wrong?

"Yes!", he finally replied. She looked up at him, with her eyes squinted, "Yes, what?", she asked.

"I considered your offer and I'm telling you, YES., however only for a couple of months. See how things go.", He replied. Ms. Rebecca smiled so hard as if she just won the lotto. She was a business woman and one thing she knew how to do was make money. And just like that, a business marriage was formed.

"Don't worry Dominique, everything that happens will be strictly confidential. There's no need to screen these ladies, because I personally know them and the last thing, they need is a scandal. Everything will be discreet. I promise.", She added. Dominique was soaking in everything she was saying. For his sake, he was hoping she was right. The very last thing he needed was another stint in the prison system.

"Are you planning on spending the night?", she inquired.

"Yeah, why not. It's not like I have a job to go to in the morning.", He answered sarcastically. They both laughed.

"Well, this calls for a celebration.", She

said opening a bottle of champagne she had by the tub. Moments later, they got out the tub and ended the night in the bedroom with another round of intense toe-curling sex.

The next morning, Dominique woke up to breakfast in bed. A stack of pancakes, 2 eggs scrambled with cheese, and turkey sausage covered the plate that Rebecca held in his face. Looking at it, Dominique couldn't remember the last time he had breakfast in bed. It had to be years, if ever. The aroma was soothing to his nose but tastier to his tongue. Rebecca watched as Dominique devoured his food. She enjoyed watching a man eat her food, to her it was like talking to his soul.

"This was good. Thanks Rebecca.", Said Dominique.

"Well, you ate that food as if it was me.", she replied with a flirtatious smile.

"Nah, the finest cuisine has nothing on

you.", He said with a quick wink. She smiled at the compliment. She was very much turned on again.

"Well you finish up. I'm going to take a shower. We have a big day ahead of us.".

As she left the room, she let her robe fall slowly to floor in front of him. She knew it would only entice him, and she was all for it. Her soft juicy ass jiggled with every step she took. Dominique was absolutely aroused, again.

As Rebecca stepped into the hot shower, she went into instant trance of tranquility as the water hit her skin, like magic little fingers. Almost immediately, Dominique walked inside the bathroom completely nude, and slid the shower door to the side, gaping at Rebecca's soapy body he joined her inside. Rebecca stepped aside so that he could have full access to the water. Once his body was fully wet, she began soaping his back. Working her way around to the front and back. She pressed her breast against his back, then reached her hands around his waistline and began stroking his already erect cock. The feeling from her soapy teasing little hands had Dominique's dick rock hard. He turned her around and gently backed her against the wet shower wall. He proceeded to turn her around and bend her over. Her ass was looking like a captivating masterpiece under the water. A work of art he couldn't resist any longer, so he plunged deep into her wetness. When all 10 inches had entered her treasure box, she tried to squirm away to release a couple of inches, but he grabbed her small waist to prevent it. His fast-hard strokes had her feeling both pain and pleasure. She couldn't contain her moans or her body's response as she started to coat his manhood with her juices. Dominique was so focused. The only thing he could hear was the sound of his stomach slapping against her ass. Then Rebecca's voice cut through his mind saying, "Slap my ass. Please slap my ass.".

He obliged slapping and leaving handprints on her tender flesh. Rebecca's legs quivered. Losing strength in her legs, on the verge of buckling, but Dominique kept that from happening by holding her up by her waist. Dominique continued surfing in her wetness, taking her to her next round of explosion, but this time it was going to be met with his.

Dominique was pounding away, not saying a word. When his body began to shake, muscles spasmed as he released himself. They came simultaneously.

Two hours later Dominique and Rebecca entered a tailor store with the intention to enhance his appearance. She knew he was going to need a slight upgrade to go from ordinary to extraordinary especially considering the prices she would set for his services. Rebecca was very sophisticated with an authentic eye for well-groomed handsome men. Every suit got tailored to perfection, and Rebecca took photos of Dominique as he modeled them in front of her. She loved how his broad shoulders and chest bulged in every suit. Dominique got a pair of shoes to match every suit and bottle of Jean-Paul Gautier cologne. They ended the shopping spree with Dominique completing his wardrobe with a Breitling watch. Rebecca felt, if Dominique was going to represent her, he had to look and smell his best.

By 3pm they were heading back to Brooklyn from Manhattan to get ready for their dinner party at Trump Plaza on 58th street.

Before exiting the car, Rebecca described what suit and shoes she wanted him to wear. Dominique couldn't have agreed more. He had the same outfit in mind.

"Be at my place by 6pm, and please be on time. I hate being late for anything.", She stated.

"You don't ever have to worry about that.", He replied. They both exited the car. He walked to the trunk and collected all of his bags and began walking to his house. Rebecca walked towards hers.

When Dominique walked inside the house and made it to the living room, he noticed his grandfather, Steward, sitting in his recliner watching Sports News. Dominique sat down on the next couch but still close, wanting to engage into a conversation with him. It had been a while with him, its either working or spending time with Rebecca.

"Hey old man. What you watching?", He asked.

"Nothing much, just listening to the critics talk bad about my Yankees.", Steward replied.

"I know it's a bad time grand-dad, but do you think I can get a moment of your time?", Dominique asked. Steward grabbed the remote and turned off the tv.

"Sure, what's on your mind, grand-son.", He replied in a concerned tone.

"Wow, I don't even know where to start.", Dominique continued.

"You can start with what's got you troubled the most.", Steward replied.

"Well, the first day I came home, I ran into Ms. Rebecca, when I was taking out the trash. She offered me a home cooked meal over at her place. Kind of like a homecoming dinner.", Dominique continued.

"Boy, I sure hope you didn't stand that fine woman up...", Steward interjected.

"No! Not at all. I had dinner with her, but one thing led to another", Dominique interrupted.

"Wait, wait, wait! Wait one minute. When you say one thing led to another, exactly what do you mean?", Steward asked.

"What I mean is that we ended up having sex.", Dominique added.

"I guess that explains all those shopping bags are over there." Steward replied, looking at the bags.

"Yeah, I guess you can say that." Dominique replied with a grin.

"And the problem is?.. Because I honestly don't see one, Dominique. You had sex with a fine older woman, and that makes you a lucky man in my book, and she's splurging on you.??? Please, help me see where the problem is, because I haven't heard one yet." Steward inquired.

"The sex is not the problem. The problem is I lost my job the other day, and I told her about it. She offered me a business proposition, which entails me having sex with other wealthy women.", Dominique did his best to explained. His grandfather looked at him in silence for what seemed like forever, with his mouth hung open. It was as if he was processing all the information his grandson just laid out for him. Finally, he said, "Hold up, grandson! You mean to tell me she's trying to turn you into a gigolo?!".

"Correct." answered Dominique. Steward began laughing hysterically. Dominique looked at his granddad confused because he didn't see what was so damn funny.

"I'm sorry grandson. I don't mean to be laughing at you, but I just still don't see the problem. You get to have sex with women and get paid for it. She obviously thinks your that good, so I say, give it a try.", said Steward.

"What do you think mom would say about this, granddad?", asked Dominique.

"Of course, your mother would never approve of it. No mother would, but at the end of the day, you got to take care of yourself. Besides, if my daughter was alive, would you have talked to her rather than me, especially about something of this nature?", Steward inquired.

"No, not at all.", Dominique answered.

"Good answer. One thing you need to understand about your grandfather, if you don't know already. I wouldn't tell you to do something, that I wouldn't do myself. Hell, if I was about 40 years younger, we would be in business together.", Steward said with a hearty laugh. Dominique, himself, laughed at the thought. He thought it was hilarious, because he just couldn't imagine it. He grandfather didn't find it THAT funny.

"WHAT?! You don't think your grandfather was that good? Back in my heyday, the women use to call me 'Sweet Dick Daddy Do Right'.", Steward said with his chest puffed out in a superhero stance. Dominique had just heard it all. He got up from the couch, laughing harder.

"I bet they did.", he said.

"Wait, where you going? I'm not done.", proclaimed Steward.

"I got to get ready. I'm going out with Rebecca tonight. Love you Granddad its always real", added Dominique. He walked away still laughing. That little conversation with his grandfather made him feel a little better about what he was about to do.

An all-black Mercedes s600 pulls up in front of the Trump Plaza. The chauffeur gets out wearing a tuxedo when he opened the door for Dominique and Rebecca. Dominique steps out first, looking quite dapper, reaching his hand inside of the car to help Rebecca out. She grabs his hand and swings her right leg out and the rest of her body follows. Dominique tucked her hand underneath his arm and began walking, making their red-carpet debut with a stylish appearance. The duo stole the spotlight and was enjoying every bit of it. The paparazzi kept the cameras on Rebecca, and she gave them model poses while Dominique stood a couple of feet behind, letting her enjoy her moment. Her sexy revealing Gucci dress was flirting with the cameras while her diamond chic chandelier earrings and platinum & diamond encrusted Bulgari Serpenti necklace was dancing from the flashes from the camera. When she felt that she gave enough photos to the paparazzi, she reached for Dominique's arm and they walked inside the majestic building. They amplified the lovely glow that cast around the room. To Dominique the function was like something out of a movie. Here it is, Dominique was confined behind concrete walls and steel bars surrounded by cold harden criminals and corrupt prison guards. The contrast between then and now was extreme. It made him feel that maybe his current surroundings were proof that his life could only prosper. The room was filled with political figures, celebrities, and socialites networking and comingling.

Inside Dominique felt like a fish out of water. He would never allow anyone to know that. He moved through the crowd like it was his event. He knew that if he could make it in prison, and in the streets of Brooklyn, then he could carry himself amongst these Ivy League grads and celebrities.

When Rebecca spotted her cougar circle, she guided Dominique toward the lion's den with her. When they approached them, Rebecca broke up their private conversation by saying, "Fancy that ladies.". They all turned around and responded in unison, "Fancy that.".

They rested their eyes on their long-time friend. They were shocked to see Rebecca not only with a man, but a man half her age. On top of that, he was BLACK. All these years of knowing her, they had never seen her with someone of the opposite sex. She was the only one that wasn't married.

"What is the topic of discussion now?", asked Rebecca.

"That's irrelevant. What's more

important is the identity of your date. Who is he?", Norah asked.

"My name is Dominique Vox.", he said reaching his hand to politely introduce himself. Norah reached her hand out to meet Dominique's.

"You can just call me Norah." she said. Dominique gently kissed the back of her hand.

"Pleased to meet you, Norah." he said.

"Your pleasure is all mines.", she said slyly. Norah flirted with Dominique right in front of Rebecca with no care in the world. Even though they were good friends, they still tried to out sexy each other. Rebecca didn't care the least, she knew Norah was going to fall for Dominique's handsomeness. Rebecca knew Norah was going to support her male escort business. She couldn't help it. Whatever Norah wanted. Norah got. That's how she was, and they were ok with that.

"My name is Ariel.", Ariel said, reaching her hand out. Dominique let go of Norah's hand and gently grabbed Ariel's and kissed the back of her hand as well. Rebecca's other friend, Camille, followed suit.

"My name is Camille, and it's a pleasure to meet you, Dominique."

He kissed her hand as well. Each one of them continued to flirt with him in their own way. They were instantly hooked by his handsome good looks, mannerisms, and Romeo charm. In their eyes, George Clooney didn't have enough style and charisma to match Dominique's. He enjoyed the attention from these sleek and chic cougars.

"Well I'm going to let you ladies catch up. I'll be back shortly.", Dominique said as he looked at Rebecca for approval, which she gave. Rebecca wasn't concerned about Dominique embarrassing her while he got acquainted with the guests. She felt that he was intelligent, confident and pleasant enough to mingle and hold his own. He was well informed about many things. He could engage and talk about matters like any politician presently in that room. Dominique knew he made his presence felt with the cougars by their aroused hospitality upon meeting them. He walked away with a confident swagger only a person can be born with. Norah turned directly towards Rebecca with an acquisitive look.

"Who's the pin up hunk?", she asked. Ariel and Camille just looked at Rebecca with a curious look on their face as well.

"I paid for him from an escort service.", Rebecca replied. Norah, Camille and Ariel exploded in laughter, not believing Rebeca one bit. They knew Rebecca was daring, fun and adventurous, but this was a bit much.

"Are you serious?", asked Camille.

"Absolutely. I'm not ashamed of it

either. Besides, that piece of flesh between his legs, reaches his knees.", Rebecca replied with a smirk.

"He puts every man in this room to shame.", she continued. Camille and Ariel jaws dropped. Norah was all smiles. That's all that she needed to hear. Her plan was playing out perfectly thus far.

Norah's mind was racing, primarily how she going to sink her teeth into Dominique that night. She planned to make him her nightcap.

Hours passed, wine, champagne and margaritas were still flowing like water. People still partied with no intention of stopping anytime soon. Dominique had just walked away from a conversation he was engaged in when he felt a tap on the back of his left shoulder. He turned around to see who it was that wanted his attention. Norah stood directly in front of him with a yearning look in her eyes and a tempting smile on her face.

"Hello Mr. Wonderful. Thought I would come over and keep you company for a while. I was just wondering to myself why a bright and attractive specimen such as yourself would want to hang around these old boring people, when you can be doing other things way less boring.", she added with a smile and a flirtatious wink.

"You know what, I was just asking myself the same question.", Dominique said, flirting back.

"Well, why don't we blow this place, and get better acquainted. My room number is 202.", she replied.

"What exactly do you have in mind.", Dominique responded.

"Let's just say I spoke with Rebecca…. I know about your services and I'm in desperate need of some company.", Norah whispered seductively in his ear.

"I would love that Norah, but my time is very valuable.", Dominique whispered bluntly, looking directly in her eyes.

"I want what I want.", Norah replied. She continued, "Let's cut the small talk. The way I look at it, we're all selling ourselves for something, so what's your price?".

"Five thousand is the going rate for first time customers.", Dominique responded as he quickly glanced around the room, then back to Norah with a serious look on his face. Norah laughed to herself she was getting a deal. Especially, if he stood up too all the hype Rebecca was laying out. Norah hoped that he was solid enough to handle her. She had a large sexual appetite. She handed him her room key.

"I'll see you in an hour.", she said, and just like that she walked away blending into the crowd. Dominique pulled out his cellphone and began texting Rebecca to update her on what was going on and with who. She texted him back:

Norah's husband won't catch on. He will be too occupied. In very good hands.

Dominique laughed to himself after reading it. Knowing what Rebecca meant by "Good Hands". He had been in her "good hands" at times himself. He could appreciate how blissful Norah husband's night was going to be. Dominique continued to mix and mingle with the crowd to kill some time.

Dominique stepped off the elevator with sex on his mind. Something was telling him being with Norah was going to be adventurous. There was something in her persona that exuded desire. He finally came upon Room 202. He slid the key card into the lock and a green light lit. As he walked inside, he was greeted by dim lights and soothing sounds of slow music. He removed his jacket and draped it over the arm of the couch. Removing a bottle of Metaphora wine from the ice bucket he filled two glasses and sat down. As he sipped on his glass Norah stepped out of the bedroom with a devilish smile on her face. A Victoria's Secret Red sequin bra and panty set covered her skin as her body seductively swayed with the rhythm of the music. The beat caused her ass cheeks to undulate in the most arousing manner. Her double D rack bounced around in a come touch them way. Norah was a natural. It was never forced, she was extremely confident and blithely comfortable with nudity. Watching her use her entire body to entice him was mesmerizing. Dominique had to admit, Norah's body looked gorgeous and limber for her age. It was toned and sculpted. Dominique could tell that fitness was definitely a part of her daily regimen. He laid back on the couch and enjoyed every second of the explicit show he was witnessing. The show caused Dominique to experience a rise in testosterone and adrenaline. When Norah got within a few feet of him, she began crawling on the floor like a cat in heat. By the time she reached Dominique he already had his dick out. Norah eyes lit up with amazement. The size of his appendage was breathtaking. It was a huge difference from her pencil dick husband. Although impressed, she wasn't a bit intimidated. She was like a kid in a candy store. Just that fast, she buried her face in his lap and slowly began lubing him up with her tongue. His huge cock went down her throat smoothly without her gagging. As she's sliding her mouth back and forth, he put his hands on the back of her head and starts thrusting his hips in the rhythm of her warm wet mouth. Her no gag reflex had Dominique in such a sexual serenity, he let go of her head and laid back enjoying the royal ride. She sucked his dick like she was trying to salvage her reputation. He was trying to hold on from cumming, but Norah's blow job was giving him no choice in the matter. Her mouth game was so mind blowing, that Dominique busted off with intensity and without warning. His orgasm graffitied the walls of her throat and she swallowed every drop, leaving none to waste. When he gained feelings back into his legs, Dominique got up, helping Norah off her knees. He threw her on the couch, putting her in a doggie position. He began pulling his pants and boxers down to his ankles. She wasted no time grabbing and maneuvering his dick into her pussy. He penetrated her so deeply that she instantly began to tremble. It was in this moment she realized that she underestimated the size of his man meat. Dominique started pounding her pussy aggressively and slapping her ass in the process. She was loving every minute of it. The unnecessary roughness turned her on. There was nothing that turned her on more than getting sexually bullied.

"Harder!", she screamed. "Fuck me! Oh God, fuck me harder you fucking dinosaur, please!"

And that he did. In the process, he invaded her anal vault with his thumb like a butt plug to double the pleasure. With every stroke he shoved his thumb in and out thoroughly and properly, stretching her and she was loving the abuse. From the anal acrobats combined with Dominique working her, Norah came in no time.

"Oh- my- god! Oh- my- god!", she yelled as she climaxed. Norah fell to the couch in a missionary position with a steely glare in her eyes. He wasn't done with her yet. Dominique placed both her waxed legs on his shoulders, while placing both his hands around her throat, slightly choking and then began fucking her with the same rhythm from the last position. The intensity from the choking and Dominique long strokes had Norah on the verge of exploding again. He slowed down his strokes and began to thrust slow and hard. Norah climaxed. The orgasm came crashing like water on a shore. Dominique busted right after her. They both fell asleep.

Meanwhile, Rebecca had Norah's significant other Dennis blindfolded and tied up, tongue fucking her pussy and asshole like he was in a suckfest. The feeling felt amazing to her. Rebecca grinding her firm tight ass on his face while giving him a hand job. He always had a thing for Rebecca. He asked her can he fuck her prior to this day, but Rebecca always politely declined. He was shocked, yet ecstatic when she finally allowed him too this time. Well sort of. He was a little disappointed that she didn't allow him to penetrate her with his dick but was satisfied with her allowing him to perform oral, which he knew he was good at. Dennis didn't care too much about the rejection once Rebecca agreed he can suck her toes, pussy and asshole. Actually, he didn't mind because that's always been a fetish of his. It made it easy for him to eat her pussy like it was a filet mignon gourmet meal. He knew his dick was small, but who cared, he had money. And in his mind, the money made up for his lack of size.

Rebecca on the other hand enjoyed the way his thick tongue went in and out her pussy like a pair of fingers. The suction from his lips on her made her body shake. The powerful sensation took over her and she had no choice but to surrender to a squirting climax. She helplessly used his face as a cum target, drenching his face with her sweet nectar. He been trying to fuck her for years and she never allowed it. He was rich, but always seemed like a bore. The sight of his small dick almost made her change her mind and decline again. She felt bad for Norah, who was stuck having full intercourse with him. Before she left him in his hotel room, she had him pay her for the privilege of making her cum. She couldn't wait to get back to Dominique. She wanted that. She needed that. Desperately.

The next afternoon, Norah woke up to a big ole plush empty bed. She wondered if Dominique left. She knew he had to by the piece of paper resting on top of the pillow where his head was supposed to be. She grabbed it, read it and dialed his number. After two rings Dominique answered the phone, he had already started his day.

"Hey Dominique, it's Norah. I'm just calling to let you know I had a wonderful time last night and I hope you did too.".

"Sure did.", he replied.

"I never felt so liberated in my life.", she continued.

"Thank you. Good to know I did my job.", Dominique said through a smile.

"I also had a wonderful time.", he added.

Norah smiled inside, feeling satisfied that she took care of a stud like Dominique. The last time she had good dick like that it was battery operated.

"Dominique, one other thing.", Norah continued slyly.

"Yeah, what's that Ms. Lady.", he responded.

"I would like to keep this strictly confidential.", she said in a slight whisper, as if someone was listening.

"You don't have to ever worry about that. I couldn't agree with you more", he said reassuring.

"That even goes for Rebecca. I would really prefer her to stay out of my business.", Norah stated with sternly.

Dominique was caught off guard with the request. He wasn't sure where she was coming from, especially seeing how it was Rebecca who hooked it up. Now, she was asking him not to tell Rebecca. Who did she think he would be splitting the money with?

He knew in his gut he should be honest with Norah, but he doesn't want to ruin the start of something profitable. All he could do is truly hope that not being honest with Norah wouldn't cause issues later.

"I understand.", said Dominique.

"Good to know we both agree on that.", Norah replied with a sigh of relief.

"Now, what was so important that you had to leave a willing naked woman in bed by herself?"

"I'm at the gym trying to sweat out last night alcohol.", he answered coyly.

"Why? You miss me already?", he asked with a smile.

Norah smiled at Dominique's sweet charming question. It made her blush. She couldn't deny the fact he was so right.

"Yes, I do miss you, but that's not the reason I asked you that. Oh really? Look Dominique, what you doing later, because I do have something to give you for the wonderful time last night."

"I'm not really doing much after", he replied.

"Good! So that means you can meet me around 6 o'clock.", she added with excitement.

"I'm perfectly ok with that.", Dominique replied.

"Are you familiar with Merchants on 61th and First Ave?", she asked.

"Perfect place to meet up. I'll be there at six.", He said assuring. Dominique completely lied about knowing the location. He just wanted her to think he be in the right circles. Plus, he figured it shouldn't be that hard with Google.

"So, I'll see you then."

"You betcha.", responded Dominique.

They both hung up their phones with the intentions of making room in the rest of their day to meet up. Dominique had to admit to himself, Norah was one hot cougar. She was intelligent and extremely sensual. Dominique liked that.

What caught his attention instantly was the sight of a well-rounded bubble butt practically busted the seams of white stretch pants she wore. It was almost as if they were painted on. Her black thong was clearly visible. This woman was blessed with a natural hourglass figure. She rocked skimpy pink wife beater. She had a white sports bra underneath, but it didn't help much because every time her feet touched the treadmill, her luscious, perky breast swayed to the movement. Sexiness exuded from every one of her pores. The way the gym lights glisten off her sweaty body could be mistaken for a treasure box being opened showcasing flawless diamonds. Her silky smooth complexion was like soft caramel... Her skin looked incredibly soft. As his gaze lingered on, he spotted a feather tattoo behind her left ear, he admired the pretty ink on her neck. When she turned her head and he saw her flawless, adorable face his heart stopped. Her dreamy gloss enhanced her juicy lips, making them look succulent and soft. She was the most gorgeous brunette he had ever seen before. He thought to himself how she favored Christina Milian. Dominique was overcome with lust and savored every portion of her exotic beauty. Looking at her was enough to get his imagination flowing and his loins boiling. He couldn't control his impulses he knew he had to say something to her. So, he instantly began to strategize a way to woo her, even if it was unpredictable and funny. Whatever it was going to be he had to seize the opportunity and quickly because he was pressed for time. He had to meet Norah in a few hours, but he had to go home first and get dressed. Whatever he was going to do or say, it had to be done fast. She just stepped off the treadmill and was walking in his direction. His adrenaline started rushing, he couldn't find a way to articulate his feelings, but there was still no way in hell he was going to let her get away. When she was within a few feet of him Dominique stepped in front of her with both hands raised like he was surrendering to something greater than him, in all actuality, he was surrendering to her beauty. She turned off her iPod and took out one of her earbuds to hear why this total stranger wanted her attention. She didn't feel threatened by his demeanor, so she decided to give him an ear.

"I don't mean to impose on your workout, but I think you are extremely beautiful.", Dominique began charmingly. Against her will her cheeks became a little flushed with a pinkish hue. She refused to smile determined not to let this handsome smooth-talking stranger manipulate her.

"Thank you, that's sweet of you.", the young lady responded.

"No thanks needed I'm only speaking the truth, and real truth never hurt nobody."

"Are you always this "truthful" with all the ladies?", she asked with a hint of sarcasm on her tongue. Amused by her response and turned on by her expression Dominique smirked and replied, "No, not at all it is not every day I get to see a rare beauty such as yourself."

The young lady gave him the side eye indicating that she wasn't falling for any of that game he was playing. She wasn't going to give him the benefit of doubt because he has got to earn that. So, she figured she'd give him a challenge to see if he deserved her attention, and if he did and could keep it, he might have a chance, but He was going to have to bring more than a handsome face and a nicely built body to the table. Even if she was attracted to him. From a distance stranger passing by could clearly see the obvious sparks between them.

"You may fool some people most of the time but can't fool genuine people all the time. Only fools do and say foolish things ending up in messy situations. Let me be the first to tell you, I am far from a fool… Please excuse my lack of respect, my name is Dominique", he continued extending his hand to properly introduce himself. Returning the gesture, she took his hand replying, "Nice to meet you. My name is Cara."

"That's a nice name. Cara? Like Cara Lee Rice?", Dominique queried.

"Why yes, yes, it is.", Cara said clearly impressed she continued, "I never realized that, thanks for bringing it to my attention.

"What's your nationality Cara?", Dominique asked.

"I'm Hawaiian and Cherokee Indian.", Cara informed.

"See, I knew it thank you for proving me right. That is a unique combination. Making you the rare beauty I knew you were.", he said continuing to thickly lay on his charm. Cara gave him the same bashful smirk that she had blessed him with moments before. Dominique couldn't help but notice her enticingly provocative green eyes, as the sun shimmered off them like a jewel. They ended their conversation and walked to their respective locker rooms. They both showered and dressed in their street clothes. Once Dominique finished making himself presentable, he stood at the entrance of the female locker room waiting for Cara to exit. After about 15 minutes of waiting he realized that she must have finished before him and left. Dominique headed out front toward his waiting Uber. Although he shrugged it off as a loss, he still was a little bit disappointed, as he had hoped to continue their conversation. As Dominique reached the sidewalk in front of the gym an all-black BMW-M5 pulls up with Adorn by Miguel blasting from its speakers. "Are you ok? You were in there for a long time. I was beginning to think maybe you drowned in the shower. I was starting to worry", Cara teased sarcastically.

"Aww that's cute. You've only known me for a few minutes, and you're worrying about me.", Dominique retorted in jest.

"Don't flatter yourself. I was just curious as to what was going on with you in there, that is all.", she politely checked him with an attractively devious sneer.

"Well, thank you for being concerned.", Dominique chuckled.

"That's the least I could do.

Especially for someone who has made my day. I have to say your compliments and confidence was a breath of fresh air."

"Hmmm, I'm glad I was able to make your day a little brighter. I would love for you to make my day.", He seduced.

"And how would I do that?

Going in for the kill, Dominique said, "By giving me your number so that we can continue to get to know each other.".

"Uhhh, Sorry nope.", Cara said slightly apologetically. Taken back by her refusal Dominique was completely confused. He thought he had this in the bag. After all, the vibe she was emitting led him to believe she was feeling him. As his mind nonchalantly dissected their entire encounter she interrupted, "But.... I'll take yours."

Dominique nodded with a feeble smile and recited his digits and she logged it into her contact list. Before pulling off Cara assured him that she would be in contact. Dominique stood in place and watched until her tail lights were no longer visible. He then walked to his Uber. He did not want her to see him getting into a cab. As far as he was concerned, that would have been a blemish on his masculinity. Seeing Cara's BMW really tugged at Dominique's pride. Shaking his head, he thought, "I really need to get my shit together. I can't be trying to bag females with nothing on my plate. It's time to find new game and play it hard. I need to get my stacks up and rebuild my image."

When Norah got off the phone with Dominique, she laid back on the bed lusting for him. She grabbed a fluffy plush pillow placed it between her legs, closed her eyes, and reminisced about yesterday's events. She recalled every glorified detail and every moment was revitalizing. The spontaneous anal exploration was complete ecstasy. She couldn't believe that something so dirty and taboo could be so gratifying. When Dominique breached her asshole with his thumb, it ignited a craving for that sensation. She loved the feeling but hated the action. It left her vulnerable. For a complete stranger to have so much power and control over her body and mind made her feel inadequate. Norah was a strong, dominant, independent woman who was obsessed with being in control. She felt as if she lost all control in that hotel room to Dominique. Dominique dicked her in to a dizzy spell. Leaving her exhausted in a fetal position sucking her thumb. Something she hadn't done since she was four. Norah didn't feel bad about her tryst with Dominique. It had been years since she has felt loved and valued by her husband. Their marriage was devoured by the never-ending list of call girls. Norah's husband had an immense sexual appetite problem he was never hungry for her. His sexual escapades and empty promises drained Norah making her emotionally numb. She was tormented by self-doubt and depression. Dealing with these unwelcomed conditions led her to imagine extremely violent thoughts where her husband was concerned. She did have a few fond memories of her husband still lingering around from when they were devoted to each other. However, that was many years ago. In the political circle and the public eye, they were a perfect couple, and her husband was a perfect gentleman in every sense of the word. Many considered him to be one of kind; decent compassionate, and just an all-around wonderful human being. Behind the curtains, he was a miserable, mean, and heartless person. Norah snapped herself out of her distraught haze filled with the thoughts of all her husband's infidelities. She despised the moment she allowed her husband and the pain he had inflicted invade her mind. She got out the bed, freshened up, and left the hotel.

Norah entered her beautiful home with her husband nowhere in sight. She knew that he wasn't going to be home. She called his cell phone twice and his office once. Where ever he was at, she honestly didn't care. Not answering his phone and constantly being absent from home gave Norah more of reason to carry on with her plans with Dominique. Norah went to grab something to drink from the fridge where she found a note from her husband Dennis.

OUT OF TOWN ON BUSINESS FOR A FEW DAYS-DENNIS.

Read the note. Years ago, this news would have been heartbreaking and disappointing. Now it was music to her ears and very exciting. As soon as she had completed reading the note, she involuntarily imagine Dennis and his personal assistant in a hotel room somewhere shacked up. Norah shook the image out of her head, took a sip of her drink and headed up the stairs. She showered to wash off Dominique's scent from earlier that day so that she could replace it with a fresh application. After an hour of pampering and moisturizing her skin to perfection she got dressed, got in the car, and exited the gates of her home.

Meanwhile, Dennis was in the middle of another conquest. This time, her name was Lynda. They were enjoying each-others' company on his private jet. They were only an hour away from Miami, and even though they were both anxious to reach their destination, they still didn't want to rush it. Especially not Dennis. He enjoyed every position he had the little cunt in. As Lynda straddled his cock in the reverse cowboy position, Dennis laid back watching her ass bounce up and down on his dick. She rode him ferociously. She was determined to cum no matter what. His little dick wasn't helping the matter. It was nowhere near her g spot. You would have thought he would have at least ate the pussy, but his spiteful privileged ass only cared about his own pleasure, especially since it was on his dime. She was making him pay for her time considerably with absolutely no mercy on his bank account.

Norah eagerly awaited Dominique's arrival to the secluded area in the rear of the restaurant. The spot was perfect for their discretion. A perk of the restaurant's V.I.P guests. Norah reserved the special section with a confidential table. She had to maintain her anonymity. Although she could care less about her marriage, she was determined to keep her name and reputation intact. At this point, Dominique, was 30 minutes late. Norah was becoming extremely irritated. She could never understand tardiness. She hated not being on time and hated when people wasted her time. The waitress approached to offer her services for the second time, but this time Norah accepted. She ordered a chill bottle of Dom Perignon to calm her nerves a bit. After a ten-minute wait, the waitress returned with the bottle and two chilled glasses. She did this knowing that Norah was seated alone. This oversight or deliberate taunt only aggravated Norah more. She was sipping on her third flute, when she finally noticed the hostess escorting Dominique over to her table. Although he was a bit more than fashionably late, her mood immediately shifted once she saw him. He had a sexy swagger that aroused her. This black man exuded strength and sophistication mixed with a sort of bad boy rebel appeal, which had her craving any amount of time he was willing to spare.

Dominique walked into the restaurant commanding attention with his high confidence and cool demeanor. He was dressed for the occasion. He always kept in mind the few jewels, Ms. Rebecca, had bestowed upon him. Lending her expert eye to assist in elevating his look. He had to admit, he appreciated her advice, and the public response has been very beneficial. He knew his image was important, and thought he had that locked, however the few minor changes that was suggested, truly changed the game. He noticed how people reacted to his presence, and he loved it. He saw Norah seated at the table as the hostess escorted him over to her. Once he reached the table, he sat down explaining why he was late. He thought it was only right. He grabbed her hands, looked her straight in the eyes, and began, "I'm truly sorry I'm so late. The train station was kind of hectic. There was a 25-minute delay for some reason, and I had no reception underground to give you a call. I hope you could find it in your heart to forgive my lack of punctuality. Please tell me how I can make it up to you?".

When Norah looked into Dominique's eyes, she saw his sincerity and genuine honesty. She saw someone who cared about her time, or at least pretended to be. Either way the gesture and effort were recognized and appreciated. It had been a long time since anyone gave enough energy to make her think they were at least trying. It was such a rare occurrence, that it felt somewhat bizarre. Besides, how could she resist all that sexiness.

"No worries, my dear. The train was out of your control; however, I can think of a few ways you could make it up to me…", Norah purred.

"But we can discuss that later", she added. smiling, she reached into her purse and pulled out a thick envelope. Discreetly, she slid the envelope across the table. It was the five thousand, as promised. He smoothly placed the envelope with the cash inside the blazer's inner pocket. This little transaction solidified that more freaky fucking was in order. However, the night played, one thing he knew for sure, it was going to be mutually beneficial. Dominique took the champagne bottle and refilled Norah's glass, then poured himself one. They both raised their glasses to a toast.

"I would like to make a toast to a promising, stimulating, and wonderful night to come", said Dominique.

"I know that we've already spent an amazing night together, but I promise tonight will be even greater. I also promise that not to sabotage the morning by disappearing...", he added smoothly.

"You better not!", Norah exclaimed. Glasses kissed as they shared a laugh.

Soon after, the waitress approached to take their orders. Dominique ordered the grilled chicken and broccoli alfredo, along with garlic bread and a side salad covered with Caesar dressing. He wanted to make sure he had a hearty meal. The last "date" he went on was with Ms. Rebecca, and though it was tasty, it was a snack to a grown ass man Besides, with the nights coming events, he was definitely going to need all the energy he could muster. Norah, on the other hand, ordered something light, garlic shrimp salad with avocado dressing. She figured she would save room for the main course back at the hotel. Handing their menus to the waitress, they continued their conversation, as she walked away. While they were talking, enthralled in each other's company, Dominique's eyes began to trace down her neck slowly till they settled onto her well sculptured, plump and glistening breast. Her cleavage played a seductive game of Reveal/Conceal, in her low-cut Christian Dior blouse. It was clear that she wasn't wearing a bra. Her breast wasn't in any need of support anyway. They were naturally firm and perky. They were incredibly soft and squeezable, that he last recalled. There was so many provocative thoughts running through Dominique's mind. With each tease and please moment was saturated with lust. Unbeknownst to them two hours flew by and they eagerly finished their glasses of champagne, then left the restaurant.

While waiting for the valet to bring Norah's midnight blue Panamera Porsche, Dominique slid in front of her. He began kissing her neck and firmly palming her ass underneath her full length grey and white mink coat. The bystanders were secretly amused by the public display of affection these two was displaying. Two perfect strangers, they appeared to be a newly happy couple in love. The sound of Norah's engine purring by the curb beside them forced them to cease their intimate lock. Closing the doors of the Porsche only made Norah's panties wetter. She couldn't drive fast enough to get to the hotel and get naked.

Rebecca and Dennis met up finally at the Loews hotel in South Beach. He could have afforded to take her to a classier hotel but feared they would be noticed more. Truthfully, Rebecca preferred it this way. She didn't want to get caught in the middle of a scandal. Not only was she sleeping with a married man, but she knew his wife quite well. Dennis was also a rising political figure. She knew there was no way of getting around a rumor like that and her professional career, along with everything she worked so hard for her entire life would be in ruins.

The room was nice. It wasn't the Ritz by no means, but it had everything Rebecca needed to handle Dennis. She envisioned the room as a central place to plot and scheme a large amount of money out of him. Her plans involved sexual acrobats with no disturbances. Her goal was to work him until his soul demanded sleep. While Dennis headed to the bedroom to unpack, Rebecca- slid into the bathroom. As soon as she closed the door, she very discreetly called Dominique to check on how things were going down with Norah. She couldn't get through. The phone continued to ring until the voicemail picked up. She attempted several times to no avail. The unanswered calls threw Rebecca off her game for a moment. She slammed the phone down and began to gaze at herself in the mirror. Thoughts of Dominique and Norah's sexual escapade was scrambling her emotions and clouding her motives for the night's event.

The phone on the nightstand was ringing and vibrating continuously for several minutes until it stopped. It couldn't be heard under the sounds of what was coming from the bathroom. The running water from the shower and Norah's loud moans blocked out any type of outside interference. Dominique had Norah bent over with her head facing the wall. Her ass was elevated in the air, as he plowed her with some deep, forceful thrust of his lower body. The sound of his body hitting hers was…. Norah was ecstatic that she was finally getting the type of aggressive anal fucking she was craving. Reaching behind her and grabbing his ass and thighs, she motivated him to continue as she groaned in pleasure. She began to beg for more sexual abuse, "Oh my God! Harder…. Just like that…..Deeper...Give me all of it……..!".

Her pleasurable screams were taking Dominique to ecstasy. After about four more minutes of pleasurable pain, they both came in unison. Norah felt a warm explosion in her ass, which only heighten her orgasm. Dominique slithered out of her to apply a small but generous amount of his cum all over her ass. He laid it on thick. Once they both regained control of their bodies, following that untamed rapture, they began washing each other off. He began to massage her breast and nipples until they were as hard as push pins. Norah's light touches turned into long strokes on his well-endowed throbbing thick muscle. Dominique caught her off guard by scooping her up in his arms like a toy doll. He stepped out the shower and carried her over to the awaiting bed. He gently laid her across the plush bed. Norah's eyes filled with lustful yearning, as she stared at his broad shoulders and bulging biceps. In her eyes, she was just so amazed how his body was built to perfection and couldn't get over his huge dick. She was flabbergasted by how each and every one of his body parts complimented the other. Norah laid back and teasingly placed her baby soft feet on his masculine chest and slowly moved them down his chiseled abs. Dominique gripped both her slender ankles and began kissing them softly. He kissed her inner ankles, slowly working his way up to her inner thighs. He slowly brushed his lips and nose against her crotch area. Norah arched her back slightly and a light moan escaped her lips. Her pussy was all warmed up, nice, wet and her clit ripened to the size of a cherry tomato. It was absolutely ready for some royal treatment. Dominique wasn't trying to rush anything. He concentrated on pleasing her. Norah began biting her bottom lip and her breathing became heavy and fast, as she enjoyed every moment. As soon as he got close to her perfectly shaved pussy, he buried his tongue in her pussy and tongue fucked her like a vibrator. The moistness from his tongue and the wetness from her pussy caused a slurping sound. Norah's pussy had a sweet taste to it. The sweetness encouraged him to want more. She tried to squirm away, however Dominique had his arms clutched around her legs. When he worked the way to her clit, it sent Norah over the edge. She moaned loudly with ecstasy. She grabbed the back of his head as she began to thrust her hips against with his rhythm as she began to fuck his face. Dominique continued with his turbo tongue, not stopping the momentum until her raging water flowed like a busted faucet.

She began to feel ripples in her whole body. Ripples that made her feel powerless. She had an orgasm so strong, her heart felt like it was going to come out her chest. It was a feeling she never felt before. "Oh my God, that was amazing." She gushed.

Meanwhile, back in Miami, at the hotel, Rebecca was on the bed missionary style. Screaming and moaning, as if Dennis was killing her with his miniscule penis. He was grinding hard. Giving it everything he had. At least he thought so. He honestly didn't give two shits if the bitch was satisfied or not. He was rich. He was entitled. As long as he was able to bust off, was all that mattered. And according to him, the bitch better give an Oscar performance for him to achieve his goal.

The dick was trash, Rebecca thought to herself. No matter how much pumping Dennis was doing, it still wasn't enough according to her. She faked it to stroke his ego. On the inside she was full of giggles. The only reason she got wet in the first place was by thinking of Dominique's black massive thick cock. She couldn't wait for Dennis to cum so he could get off her and she could go take a shower. The thought of washing his pathetic sweat off her body was a welcomed thought. The fact that she couldn't get over Dominique not answer her phone calls was starting to eat at her as well. Dennis continued to pound away until he finally was on the verge of cumming. She began to egg him on.

"Come on and cum for Mama!" ... "right there…. you're the man, baby.".

As she squeezed and smacked his ass so

hard that she literally left-hand prints. The acceptable pain caused him to attempt to go deeper. His long strokes turned to short rapid thrust. His body began to tense up and he finally released…....He collapsed on top of Rebecca, as waves and waves of cum exited his body into his condom. He was momentarily paralyzed as his limp body completely pressed down on hers due to his ejaculation. The potent tide faded, and he gained back control of his body, he rolled off her breathing hard and staring up at the ceiling. After a few seconds, he dozed off snoring. Rebecca got up from the bed unsatisfied and pissed that her time was wasted. If it wasn't for his healthy bank account, she wouldn't even be bothered with him or his pathetic cock. She grabbed her phone that was nestled under her pillow and took it with her into the bathroom. She tried dialing Dominique's number again, but only ended up with the same result. No Answer. Now the voicemail was full. They haven't seen or spoken to each other since the dinner party and it was really making her vexed. Rebecca hopped in the shower to not only pamper her skin, but to wash away Dennis's strong repugnant scent off her. She was annoyed all around.

Dominique and Norah didn't get out the bed until early afternoon, the day after. After they both took a shower, Norah treated him to a nearby restaurant. They talked about a lot of things while enjoying their lunch, however the one thing that puzzled her was the reason he didn't have a car. When she asked him, he gave some lame excuse. She knew a lie when she heard one, especially with years of experience dealing with her lying ass husband. You would of thought someone with his caliber wouldn't dare be caught without a ride. Norah felt that if they were going to be having these sexual business meetings, then he is going to need a ride, in order to be prompt. She really hated tardiness. That was her pet peeve. Timing was very important to her and there was nothing punctual about the public transportation system! She made a decision. As soon as they finished their meal, she announced that she had a surprise for him. They left the restaurant in Norah's Porsche and ended up at the Range Rover dealership. As soon as they pulled up in the dealership, Dominique had some sort of idea of what that surprise was. She parked the car and turned off the engine, then turned her full attention to him.

"There are two reasons why I brought you here. First, I truly feel that a Range Rover Sport fits your style perfectly. And one thing I do know is style…", she began.

"A Range Rover man, huh?", he interrupted.

"Range Rover Sport. There is a difference.", she clarified while waving her index finger at him as if she was scolding.

"And yes, I think so.", she continued. "The second reason is for assurance"

"Assurance?", replied Dominique.

"Yes, my dear. Assurance that when I call you, there should be no reason you can't get to me when I need you and of course, *on time.*", she said through a smile on her face and winked her right eye.

Dominique smirked at the inside joke. He thought it was very assertive and tactful, which was a complete turn on for him.

"I have no issues meeting your demands. But I do have one myself.", Dominique bargained. Norah had a perplexed look in her eyes. She was curious as to what his demand could be. In her eyes, he didn't seem like the type to not just jump all over the new car idea, but he was up there trying to bargain. Could it be that she read him wrong?

"Oh really, and what might that demand be?", she inquired.

"Yes really, I only ask that we just respect our time together as well as our time apart. Simply our time together is our time together and our time apart, is what it is...apart. No last-minute escapades and please let's always plan ahead.", he laid it all out. He was grateful for the car, however he had to remind Norah that this thing they had going was business.

"Okay, that seems reasonable.", Norah agreed verbally, however in her mind she was not going to let that happen. She figured that he would never have time for another woman, if she had the money for his time. Once they both agreed to their terms, they got out the vehicle and went to get him that Range Rover.

Buzz, buzz, buzz. Cara was in her kitchen washing dishes when her front door began to buzz. The rapid sound drew her attention from the sink to the front door. She already knew who it was because only her best friend April popped up unannounced. She's the only one allowed to do so. Cara and April are childhood besties. They grew up together, and their friendship only grew stronger throughout the years. They were more like sisters. You couldn't separate one from the other.

Buzz, buzz, buzz...Cara heard the door ring the first time. She just wanted to wash and dry the last dish in the sink.

I'm coming!", she screamed. She began

walking towards the door, drying her hands off. When she opened the door, April stepped inside.

"What took you so long?", April asked.

"I was in the kitchen. Why didn't you just use the key I gave you? Ringing down my bell like you the damn police…", Cara replied pretending to sound annoyed. They both cracked up laughing and embraced. Their bond was so real. They spoke on the phone almost every day. They hadn't seen each other in four days, which felt like four weeks to them. It was time to play catch up. Cara didn't have the opportunity to tell April about Dominique yet. She definitely wanted to but didn't want to do it over the phone. This was more of a face to face type of conversation. Cara hadn't been with anyone since the love of her life, Kevin, who broke her heart for the last time. They had an off and on relationship due to Kevin's very disrespectful behavior. No matter how calculating and manipulating Kevin was, he always found a way to weasel his way back into her life. That all changed once Cara found out about the chick Kevin impregnated during one of their "on" seasons. That permanently broke her. She wasn't about to be nobody step mother in this type of fashion, and she sure as hell was not into any baby mama drama. The girl he got pregnant was the one that contacted her and was ghetto as hell. Kevin's karma would be having to deal with that lady for 18 years. Cara broke it off with him and moved on with her life. This was two years ago. April tried hooking her up with other men, however they never worked out. Cara was fine with that. She didn't have time to waste on frivolous hookups that led to nowhere. Plus, she really needed to build up her trust when it came to men. For some reason meeting Dominique sparked something in her. She couldn't figure out what it was, but all though she had not spoken to him since getting his number, she couldn't stop thinking about him. He had her very curious. She liked it.

April proceeded to sit herself down at the kitchen table. She loved when her and her bestie played catch up. She could tell something was up with Cara before Cara even told her what it was. She felt the shift in Cara's spirit, and she just knew it was good, because she hadn't felt her friend's spirit uplifted like this in a long time since her dip shit ex-boyfriend. That bastard was the anti-Christ. The emotional roller coaster he always had Cara on, made April strongly dislike him. She was extremely happy when Cara finally dropped him, however she was saddened behind the circumstances. He didn't have to do her friend that dirty. She hated when her friend was hurt. That was her sister. When Cara was hurt, she was hurt. And vice versa.

"So, what's new?!", April cooed as she crossed her legs and got comfortable.

"Oh, nothing much. Just taking in this beautiful weather, got my coffee right this morning, met a man at the gym the other day, finally decided on this room color I been....", Cara started to spill.

"Repeat that part about the man at the gym", April interrupted.

"Oh, okay...just met a guy at the gym. No biggie.", Cara said smiling confidently.

"Yes, biggie, since you over here smiling from ear to ear. I feel like a kid under the Christmas tree waiting to open my gift in the small box. The tea is hot, and I need you to pour it.", April said anxiously.

"Ok...ok....ok. So, I met this guy at the gym the other day. Extremely handsome...nice physique...and very i-n-t-e-r-e-s-t-i-n-g.", Cara dragged the last word "interesting" as she wiped both corners of her mouth with her fingers simultaneously.

"Well he sounds very "interesting.", April replied. They both busted into laughter.

"You sound like you like him. Do I need to do a background check?", April poked in jest.

"No, no need for the background check, especially since I haven't called him yet.",

Cara answered.

"You haven't called him? Why not? And why hasn't he called you yet?", April inquired.

"He hasn't called me, because I never gave him my number. I haven't called because, I don't know. I kinda don't know what to say. Plus, I don't want to seem…. desperate.", Cara said solemnly and slightly embarrassed.

"Cara, you can't think like that. Just call the man. You not asking for marriage. You're asking to get to know him, like he wants to get to know you. Maybe get some food, some drinks, and then some…. you know.", April said with a wink. They both laugh.

"Your disgusting. Ain't nobody thinking about that man's penis. Can I just get to know him first? At least a last name. Is that okay with you?", Cara replied through her tears of laughter.

"Yes, that's okay with me. But how you're going to get to know him, well at least his last name, if you don't CALL him? Just asking for a friend.", April said sarcastically.

"Point taken.", Cara stated.

"I'll give him a call later." she continued.

"No, you're going to give him a call NOW, and then you're going to give me a call LATER and spill some more tea if you happen to get any.", April said rubbing her hands together, smiling, as she proceeded to get up from the table.

"We'll talk.", she added.

"Where you going?", Cara asked.

"Going to meet up with Mike.", April replied as she walked toward the door. Mike was an Investment Banker, whom April had been dating for a couple of months. The few times Cara met him, she could tell he was a good match for her bestie. She could tell April was happy with him by the way she lit up whenever he was around, or his name was brought up. She was indeed happy for her friend. She wished to find someone that made her happy like that. April gave Cara a hug and a kiss on the cheek before she left. Cara pondered a few minutes on what she would say when she spoke to Dominique. She finally mustered up enough courage, thinking, *"What's the worst that could happen"*, grabbed her phone off the table and began to dial.

Dominique was on the F.D.R., in his brand new Ranger, heading back to Brooklyn. He was trying to get home and attempt to get some sleep, until his phone started ringing. He didn't recognize the number on the caller i.d. He turned down the radio in the car and answered, "Hello?".

"Hi Dominique. It's Cara. The lady you met at the gym the other day."

"No need for details. Your name was enough. I remember your name, just like I remember your beauty.", Dominique replied flirtatiously through a smile. Cara felt herself blush.

"Do you have a minute, Mr. Smooth?" she asked.

"I could always spare a moment for you, Ms. Cara.", he answered.

"Oh, that's nice. Well, where should we start? How about you tell me a little bit about yourself?", she asked nervously. Cara could feel her heart beating strongly through her chest.

"A little about myself, huh? Like what? What specifically would you like to know Ms. Cara?", Dominique answered. He wasn't going to just lay out there like an open book for her. She was going to have to turn a few pages.

Recovering from her slight anxiety attack, she decided to get straight to the point. After all, she didn't want unanswered questions to plaque wherever this situation could lead.

"Ok, so let's see...ummm, for starters, do you have a girl? Are you married? Do you have a "situation" ?? And Do you have children?", Cara said all in one breathe and then held her breath for a second, awaiting his reply.

Dominique laughed, then responded, "No, no, no and no! Damn girl, you just gonna jump right in with the interrogations, huh?".

"Interrogations? Nah, this was no interrogation. Just basic bottom line don't waste my time, questions. Very important questions, if you ask me. Those questions are the baseline for how this conversation plays out." she said in a serious tone.".

"True...true...good questions indeed. So, let me ask you a question. If I had a kid, would this be our last conversation?", he asked, a little more reserved this time.

"No, not necessarily. I just would like to know what I'm getting myself into. I honestly don't need, nor do I have the time for any baby mama drama.", Cara had to admit. She was happy that he wasn't tied to any obligations. That was a big fat plus in

114

her book. Dominique was very intrigued by her confidence. "Hey, how about I take you out tonight That way you can ask me anything you like face to face. And... maybe...I might have a few questions for you as well. If you don't mind?", he proposed.

"That sounds fair. How about Willie's Steakhouse? You could meet me there by 8. You do know the place, right?".

"I haven't been there, but I have heard of it. It's in the Bronx, right?", asked Dominique.

"Yup, it's quaint, quiet and the food is amazing. I think it would be the perfect spot for us to get better acquainted.", she confirmed.

"It's a date then. I'm looking forward to it." Dominique replied. The agreement ended their conversation. Cara smiled as she hung up the phone. She then looked at her phone, not realizing what time it was, before she set the date. She had to hop in the shower now if she had any hopes of getting there on time. She may not have to time to get her hair professionally done up, however she was going to need a Mani and Pedi. Luckily, she already had a cute little outfit in the closet that she had been dying to wear.

Dominique had really never been to the steakhouse before. He heard a lot about it, when he was behind the wall and had intended to check it out. This would be just as good of a time as any. Dominique made a detour to the barbershop to get cleaned up, before he went home to shower and prepare for his date with Ms. Cara.

Norah walked into an elegant spa, just as she had done three times a month for the last seven years. Awaiting her in the lobby were her two friends, Camille and Ariel. The two ladies huddled around a coffee table sipping on their tropical mimosas. Whining about how unhappy they were in their marriages when Norah walked up.

"Fancy that ladies.", said Norah.

"Fancy that.", the two couched ladies said in unison. Norah sat down and joined the ladies in catching up on all the social, political, tales of their unfaithful spouses, and the lists of life altering mistakes that followed after their respective walks down the aisle. That was all the women seem to talk about when they communed. Within the last few days though, Norah's perspective did a complete 360. She came to the conclusion that she was not going to cry, complain, or fight to save her marriage anymore. What for? She was only getting older and she had no more time or energy to waste. Dennis didn't care about her tears or complaints. And the only thing he was trying to save was alimony payments. Bastard. If he had an ounce of decency, he would have least called to let her know that he landed safely in Miami. Or just check to see if she was still breathing. They haven't spoken in over three days. It clearly showed his lack of concern. If he didn't care, then neither would she. Besides she was very comfortable with the financial back end of the marriage.

The ladies noticed a slight change in Norah's demeanor. She seemed more relaxed and had an obvious glow. They were already of aware of Dennis's frequent visits out of town, and normally Norah is all up in arms when he is gone. They were both curious to find out the reason behind the change. Especially with her walking around with her head higher than usual, as if they were beneath her. The ladies looked at each other with a cynical confirming glance and Ariel began to dig.

"So, Norah...what have you been up too these last couple of days?".

"Enjoying myself with no cares in the world. Just focusing more on me for a change. Getting everything, I deserve and more.", she gushed. Camille and Ariel looked at each other curiously, trying to read in between the lines. Their curiosity was evident, but Norah was not willing to comply. She was not going to share her rendezvouses between her and Dominique with anyone. She wanted him at her beck and call. His dick was too good to share.

"Sorry ladies", she thought in her head, "but find your own pleasure". Plus, she figured she wouldn't give these two bitties anything new to spew about.

"Please explain.", Ariel continued to dig. "I mean what changed since the dinner party till today that got you on a whole new plateau? Inquiring minds would like to know.", Ariel added with a grin.

"Please do tell.", Camille chirped in.

"Oh, for Christ sakes, I took up yoga.", Norah answered. Both ladies looked disappointed and annoyed. They thought they were going to hear something with a little sexual impact involved.

"Yoga?Yoga is what got you feeling yourself? Really? I been taking up yoga and I'm still mad after!", yelled Ariel.

"Well maybe you need anger management…", Norah suggested with a huge sarcastic smile on her face.

"Speaking of dinner parties and a couple of days ago, let's finish discussing the stud Rebecca showed up with. What was his name?", Camille added as she changed the subject from yoga.

"Dominique…. What about him?", she

asked a little too eagerly.

"Oh my God. The walk on that man. I can just tell he has a sweet piece of something swinging between those legs." Camille said with a giggle. "And not just because he's black or the fact that Rebecca confirmed, but I could just tell, and I wouldn't mind a taste of that." she added with lust in her eyes.

"I was just thinking about that the other day. I wouldn't mind a ride on that stallion.", Ariel piped in, almost drooling.

Norah was annoyed now. She was not about to share her situation with these two bitches, and she didn't need them pondering the thought of themselves getting what she already got either. She knew they could afford Dominique's services, but she was not willing to share. She loved the situation she was in with the no strings and nonstop fucking, and she didn't need anyone taking the attention he gave her away. Especially since she was willing to pay top notch to keep it going.

"Ladies, ladies, ladies, I'm sure there are plenty of places you could find a guy like Dominique willing to allow you to "taste that" or "ride the stallion" as you all putted.", Norah proclaimed.

"Just take your ass online and type in "back page", which I'm pretty sure at this point that you all are already very acquainted with.", Norah continued sarcastically as she got up to leave.

"How fast the time goes. Now if you ladies will excuse me, I have something constructive to do.", Norah concluded their visit.

Camille and Ariel smiles faded slowly, and mouths opened in shock and was appalled by Norah's behavior. They just stared at her as she disappeared out the building without getting her spa treatment.

"She must be menopausal.", stated Ariel to Camille.

"No, she's just being a bitch. I'm still going to find out from Rebecca about this

Dominique though.", Camille added. Something was up with Norah and she had a feeling it involved this Dominique. She noticed that night at the dinner when Norah left the party that Dominique left right after. She knew this, because what Norah failed to realize was Camille never took her eyes off Dominique. When he came over to their table at the party, she already knew she wanted to fuck him. She knew that glow that Norah gave off had to come from getting her back blown out. It was the same glow Rebecca gave off when she introduced him. Camille had a feeling some game was being played and she wanted in.

Hours later, Dominique was sitting in his truck outside of Willie's Steak House patiently waiting on Cara. She told him earlier on the phone that she was only ten minutes away. She was caught up in traffic. This was typical in New York City. It can work for you or it can work against you. Any which way, it was still a beautiful city. While Dominique was waiting on Cara, he received a call from Rebecca.

"Hey, how you doing sexy lady?", greeted Dominique.

"I'm doing fine, now that I know that you're okay.", responded Rebecca.

"Why wouldn't I be?", asked a puzzled Dominique.

"I called you several times while I was in

Miami. I was able to connect with you, so I started to get a lil concerned. I got back this morning, but I had a few things to do. I just got freed up, so I decided to call you again. If I wasn't able to get an answer from you this time, I was going to knock on your door.", Rebecca said with a slight bit of aggravation in her voice.

"I'm so sorry for worrying you. I just been extremely busy. So, you was in Miami, huh?", he asked attempting to change the subject.

"I told you I was going to put Norah's husband, Dennis, on ice. This way, you'd be able to work your magic. So, did you?", Rebecca questioned. Dominique cracked a confident smile and replied, "You know I did. Just like a professional.".

Rebecca laughed on the other end of the phone. She knew Norah was going to be the first to nip at the bait. The entire time Rebecca was in Miami playing with Dennis's wack ass, not one time did he fully satisfy her like Dominique could. She felt she was due for a proper sexual fix.

"So, what or who are you doing tonight. I'm in dire need of you.", Rebecca said in a low seductive tone.

"I'm sort of busy right now taking care of something. Tomorrow on the other hand, I could be all yours.", Dominique kindly rejected. Rebecca was shocked and slightly put off by this "polite" rejection from him. She tried to conceal her now rising temper and attitude and simply replied, "Ok. Tomorrow is fine. Well I'm not going to hold you up any longer. Take care of what you so need to take care of. You know how to find me.".

As she was about to end the call, Dominique yelled, "REBECCA!".

He had remembered something important he wanted to tell her.

"So, you changed your mind?", Rebecca asked.

"I would if I could, however I can't. I just wanted to tell you about the night of the dinner party. Norah asked me to keep you in the blind.", Dominique replied.

"And what did you tell her?", she asked again.

"I told her she didn't have to worry about that.", he replied.

"Mmmmmm…. okay. Thanks for being honest with me. For the record, ya'll "secret" is safe with me.", she stated sarcastically.

"I knew it would be. I just wanted us on the same page with this situation.", he added.

"We are.", Rebecca responded reassuringly.

"Good. I'll see you tomorrow, sexy.", he stated. And just like that, the conversation ended.

Just as Dominique pressed end on his cell phone, he spotted Cara's car entering the parking lot. She was obviously looking for a parking spot. When she located one, Dominique started his truck and drove across the parking lot parking right next to her.

"Ahem ahem!".

The sound of Dominique's voice made Cara jump. He laughed at her because she looked cute but scared at the same time.

"Hope I didn't startle you?", Dominque said apologetically.

"No, but you just scared me half to death.", said Cara

"I'm sorry, I wasn't trying to.", he replied.

"Yeah you did, but it's ok. I'll get you back.", she stated with squinted eyes.

"What was you doing anyway?", he asked.

"I was just about to call you to let you know I was here.", she replied.

"So, are you ready to go inside?", he asked.

"Yeah, why not?", she said with a genuine smile.

Dominique stepped out his truck wearing a dark blue True Religion jean suit, with a white True Religion t-shirt underneath and completed his attire with construction Timberland boots on his feet. Cara was looking out her car window, loving everything about his "thuggish" attire. She thought he looked handsome. It suited his sophisticated aura he gave off and she was impressed with how intelligent he spoke. She then turned towards her passenger seat and grabbed her Y.S.L purse, opened her car door and stepped out. She tried not to stare too long because she didn't want him to catch her checking him out. When she was completely out of the car, Dominique was able to see a true work of art. She wore an all-white Gucci denim jumpsuit that hugged her hourglass figure precisely. It made her firm, bubble butt gives off a sexy hue, and her black Louboutin pumps made her legs look shapelier. Dominique was so impressed; his thoughts became words.

"Sexy is, as sexy does.", Dominique said unintentionally aloud.

"Excuse me, what you say?", Cara responded not sure what he said.

"I said there is no better vision then you.", Dominique said as he cleaned it up. Cara blushed.

"Oh, thank you. That's sweet. You don't look so bad yourself.", she responded.

"I would look much better with you by my side.", he insisted.

"Ok, Mr. Smooth.", she retorted.

Dominique gently grabbed her hand, and they walked hand and hand through the parking lot into the restaurant resembling as newlyweds. Heads turned as they walked in. They attracted attention as if they were superstars. The host led them to their awaiting table. They stood out among the guest. Some of the old white guest who had no knowledge of the hip hop world assumed they were Jay Z and Beyoncé. The aura they gave off was so prestigious and refined that it was understandable why some onlookers would make that mistake. They both sat down to eat and have an honest, intelligent and productive conversation. They were both clearly attracted to one another but curious enough to excavate beneath the physical facade. After a few moments of reviewing the menu, they placed their orders. The waitress left them alone in their secluded corner after writing down their meal request. Dominique and Cara began gazing into each other's eyes, flirting without saying a word. Dominique loved her hazel eyes, especially the way they sparkled like stars in the candle light. He stared into them like he was trying to read her life story. Cara blushed from all the attention. She finally broke the ice by asking an innocent question hoping it could lead to more.

"So, Dominique, tell me a little about yourself.", Cara gently prodded.

"What do you want to know?",

he asked.

"Well you can start by telling me your full name, age, and what exactly it is that you do for a living.".

"My full name is Dominique Vox. I'm 30 years old, and I promote parties." He didn't want to get into specifics on what he really did just yet. So, he fabricated a little. He knew he should of came clean, but he didn't want Cara to start judging him and get turned off because of his current unconventional career path. Dominique smoothly diverted from the last question by reciting a believable lie. He turned the tables and asked her the same questions.

"My full name is Cara Campbell, and even though it's not polite to ask a women's age, I will be honest with you. I'm 30 years old as well. I work for E.M.S in Queens. I'm originally from Virginia where both my parents still live. I came to New York for college, but once I graduated, I got my job immediately and never made it back home. What about you? School...parents...".

"I'm from Brooklyn, New York. Born and raised. I never met my father, but my mother did a great job being both my parents till the day she passed away.", Dominique replied.

Cara sighed with pain and hurt for

Dominique's lost. She couldn't imagine losing her mother, who meant the world to her.

"I'm so sorry to hear about your lost.", consoled Cara.

"No, it's okay. My mother is in a better place right now. I rather her to be resting in peace, than to be here still suffering with cancer.".

While Dominique explained his lost, Cara looked into his eyes and saw genuine pain. It deeply touched her soul. Seeing and hearing Dominique reveal his deepest feelings made her feel at ease about eventually divulging some of the raw moments in her life. She knew none of her life experiences could compare to the loss of a mother. She did however find it necessary to open up about her heart broken split with her ex. After all, she wanted everything laid out on the table. She wasn't trying to have a repeat of unnecessary drama. This was the perfect time to share her secret pain.

"I was going out with this guy in college named Kevin Farrell for a year. Everything was so beautiful in the beginning. Ain't it always? I mean, he was a real charmer. Everything a girl could ask for. I honestly don't know why things began to change. When he began to change. What was once respectful became disrespectful. I tried to talk and would only be shut down with labels of being crazy, insecure or jealous. The last straw was getting a disturbing phone call from some loud ass ghetto lady claiming to be pregnant by him. This broad had the audacity to call me and attempt to put me in MY place because she was pregnant by MY man. Of course, I confronted him about it, and he lied. Claimed he doesn't even know the broad and that it could have been a prank by some of his fraternity buddies. The name calling of being crazy, insecure and jealous came again, and I always ended up apologizing to HIM. Then one day I came across him and a pregnant lady holding hands in the mall. When I approached him, he had a stupid look on his face like he didn't know who I was. She had to be about 7 months pregnant. When I asked him, this time in front of her, about their relationship, he introduced her as his fiancé. The nerve. He made it seem like I was some side chick he was screwing all along. She just stood there holding his arm, smiling. I wanted to wipe the stupid grin off the bitch face, but then what? Go to jail for assaulting some trap queen. I have never felt so humiliated and stupid in my life. I was faithful to this man.".

While telling her damaging story, she could feel the rush of emotions coming back as the memory of the event resurfaced. She tilted her head down in attempt to keep Dominique from seeing her distressful tears. She couldn't believe she was crying in front of this man. She thought after two years, she would of be all cried out, but obviously that was not the case. Dominique grabbed a napkin from off the table and handed it to her to prevent the tears from ruining her makeup.

"You are too gorgeous to be crying over some nincompoop.", Dominique attempted to comfort her. Cara busted into laughter when she heard the word "nincompoop" come out of his mouth. It reminded her of her grandmother. She used to call the bad kids in the neighborhood that. Dominique noticed that Cara had a smile that brightened up the room. People who have that kind of indubitable energy on their surroundings usually has a sparkling personality. She had charisma like no other woman he has met.

"I'm sorry if I may have ruined the night.", she apologized.

"No, not at all.", Dominique assured.

"Just don't cry. People might think I'm the cause of your distress.", he continued. He noticed that Cara had a tough exterior, but she was also in tuned with her soft emotional side. Dominique thought that was sexy. No man could resist a trait like that.

"So, what made you want to become an E.M.S worker?", he asked.

"Well, I enjoy helping those in their time of need. I knew since I was a little girl, that I wanted to be a humanitarian of some sorts. The health field always interested me, however I didn't want to be a doctor, but something close to it, without being a nurse. I don't know if that makes sense…", she stated with a weak smile.

"That makes perfect sense.", he replied. Dominique admired her spirit and personality. It matched her body and in his mind that was perfect. Not only was she beautiful, she was incredibly smart. Someone with a sense of style and substance. She was a great package.

After eating, swapping stories and giving each other advice for several hours, they left Willie's Steakhouse fully satisfied. They had chemistry from the start, but this first date just solidified their connection.

When they stepped out into the crisp winter air, Dominique let Cara get a few steps ahead, so he could check out her ass one more time before they departed. Watching her walk away would never get old to him he thought to himself. It looked perfectly round and inviting as it swayed to a silent rhythm that he played in his head. He had to tame his appetite in the parking lot because he didn't want Cara to think that was all he was after. He knew at that point it was only preparation and opportunity from there on out. This was only the beginning. Dominique did not mind having patience with Cara. She was not just another conquest. She had the potential to be that special someone. With that in mind, he was willing to move at her pace. Once they arrived at their awaiting vehicles, they stood staring at each other. As he stared into Cara's sweet and innocent eyes, he couldn't help but think how divalicious she looked. Cara began to feel the flutters of butterflies in her stomach as she lost herself in Dominique's handsome face.

"I have a confession to make.", said Dominique, breaking the intense stare. Cara continued staring into Dominique's eyes as she nodded her head giving him the cue to reveal whatever it was that was on his mind.

"I couldn't get you out of my mind since meeting you. I mean, your extremely beautiful, but after actually conversing and getting to know you, I find you extremely intelligent as well, which makes you simply irresistible.", he continued. Cara blushed.

"Wow! I don't know what to say to that", she blurted out as she was caught off guard.

"Just say that you will let me take you out again.", he replied.

"I…. ummm…".

Before she could say anything, Dominique bent over and passionately kissed her on her lips. His lips felt nice and warm against hers. It was magical. The butterflies she had slowly faded as she felt more secure by his embrace. No thoughts ran through her mind. She was just in the present. The present with just him right then and there. They both totally forgot about their surroundings. As she held his head to her face, kissing him back, they both fell back onto his truck. Dominique had her pressed up against his truck with his hands on her ass, giving it a nice long squeeze. They kissed with such passion that it appeared to be love. Cara gently pushed Dominique away after the realization that they were still in a very public setting. The parking lot. She clearly wanted to continue at her place, but this was not the message she wanted to send about herself. She became slightly self-conscious. Really liking this guy, but not wanting him to think she did this with other guys on the first date. Taking him home right now would go against her nature. Intercourse to her was something she cherished. It wasn't in her to have random sex with just any man. She had to be in a relationship. It had to mean something. She was raised with old school traditional values. She regained some resemblance self-control and he attempted regained his.

"I had a really nice time tonight, Dominique, but I really gotta go.", she said regrettably.

"It's been a pleasure, Ms. Campbell.", he replied.

Cara didn't say anything else. She just walked away, got in her car, then drove away like she had somewhere important to be. A little confused, Dominique got into his truck with his balls aching like a bad tooth. He sat in the driver's seat for a minute, pondering if he had made a bad decision kissing Cara so soon. After all, it was their first date. He decided to let her simmer over the nights event and then call her in the morning. He wanted to make sure no permanent damage was done. The sound of the phone ringing broke his trance. The caller I. D showed a number he wasn't familiar with. He answered anyway. "Hello?".

A low-pitched female voice came through the other end of the phone. "Good night, Dominique. This is Ariel. I met you at the dinner party the other day. I got your number from Rebecca. I hope I'm not disturbing you.", she replied.

"No, no, no, you're not disturbing me. How you been Ms. Ariel and how can I help you?", he asked.

"Well, I'm fine, thanks for asking, but I could be better. Actually, your presence in my hotel room could definitely help me obtain that goal, if you know what I mean? As I stated, I got your number from Rebecca, and let's just say I have a hefty envelope awaiting your arrival.", Ariel informed.

This was perfect timing. He had rather went home with Cara and preferred not to go home with a swollen dick. He figured he could release his lustful urge that Cara left him with and get paid for it in the process.

"Which hotel is that?", he inquired.

"The Hilton Grand, room 112.", she answered.

"I'm on my way.", he replied and just like that he drove away.

Immediately after Ariel hung up the phone with Dominique, she hopped in the shower. Her heart was pounding and pumped with fear. Her anxiety was an all-time high. She hoped her experience would be worth the risk of divorce if her husband found out. She noticed the change in Rebecca and then Norah, with her fronting ass, and she wanted that feeling too. She was in the shower for about 20 minutes. her adrenalin was still running on high. She stepped out the shower and found herself in front of a full-length mirror, attached to the bathroom wall. She was a bad bitch. She admired how youthful she looked at her age. She pulled her platinum blonde hair into an updo ponytail to show off her neck. She sprayed it with an exotic fruity fragrance that's so enticing that it put her in the mood for what was to come. Then she slipped into a sexy flirty short robe as the perfect finishing touch. The soft fabric against her skin made her feel very sexy and beautiful. Not to mention, hornier. The heavy knock at the door brought her right out her trance. She walked out the bathroom and across the room with her heart pounding faster and faster. She was a nervous wreck. She took a deep breath to calm her nerves, then she opened the door. There he stood. The fine sexy brother she met at the party. Dominique stepped inside. Ariel closed the door behind him and strutted away gracefully over to the mini bar in the room. He watched as she walked with her ass cheeks hanging out the bottom of her robe. He could tell that she had on no underwear. He was also pleased with the aroma she left behind her.

"Would you like a drink?", she asked as she bent over to retrieve the ice bucket from the bottom of the bar. When she bent over, the short robe raised more above her ass and freshly waxed pussy was exposed from the back. Dominique didn't say a word. He was already hard as hell in his pants. He walked up behind her pressing his waist against her ass, while she was still in her position. She could feel his huge dick through his pants. This made her pussy start to throb. As he continued to dry hump her from the back, she opened her legs slightly and arched her back. He stopped and then moved away. She was taken back. She wanted more. If that was a small taste of what was to come, she was ready for the entree. She tried to regain her composure as she went to retrieve his envelope. She handed it to him and winked. Dominique counted the money in the envelope to make sure the amount was correct, then placed the envelope on the bar table. He turned around to what was Ariel standing in full nudity. She had removed her tiny robe awaiting him to work his magic. He motioned for her to come to him. She walked seductively to him as demanded. He removed his shirt, showing his fine ass muscular chest. She could see his dick protruding through his pants. Her heart started beating fast again. She rubbed her hands slowly over his chest as if she was applying sunscreen. She lowered her hands to his abdomen and then tried to help remove his belt on his pants. Dominique stopped her hands, grabbed her shoulders slightly to make her go down on her knees. He pulled his pants down and his enormous throbbing penis stood at attention awaiting her drooling mouth. She devoured him. She had amazing head game. He held her head still as he jack hammered her throat with his dick. She gagged a little but was a trooper. She took all those inches as if she practiced for it all her life. He felt himself about to cum and didn't want to just yet. He pulled his dick from her mouth, then helped her off her knees. He needed some pussy. He was hornier since earlier and he needed to have a big release. No strings attached. Meaningless fucking to relieve his sexual frustration. His mission was to destroy her pussy, and he wouldn't stop until the mission has been completed.

"Finish making that drink.", he said in a whisper.

"What?!", she asked puzzled.

"The drink you offered me earlier,", he replied.

"Finish making it.", Ariel bent over to get the ice bucket from the bottom of the bar, as she did earlier, before he began humping her. Only this time, in the midst of bending over, she felt his big dick entering her pussy walls from the back. This made her moan out loud. The penetration was hard and fast. She felt herself orgasm just off that alone. Dominique didn't say a word. He was completely focused on keeping a steady rhythm to his strokes. The louder her moans became the more energy and stamina grew from his groin. He thought about Cara and the passionate kiss they shared. The shape of her ass and how it felt when he grabbed it during their kiss. This made him thrust harder and faster into Ariel.

"Oh, God...Oh God...I'm cumming!!", she

yelled. She began to cream on his dick. Dominique was still hard and horny. They weren't done. He let Ariel stand up and walked her over to the wall by the bar. He backed her against the wall like he had backed Cara against the truck earlier. He lifted one of her legs over his shoulder as he rammed his dick into her with such force that she felt him in her stomach. He began fucking her as deep and hard as he could. He fucked her with such intensity it was like he was trying to break his dick off inside of her. She wanted a good fuck and he was going to give it to her.

Ariel was in heaven. She had never been fucked like this before. He used and abused her body like a dirty whore, and she loved it. She understood now how women could become dickmatized. Were all black men like this? Oh my God, she's been missing out. It felt as if he was stretching her pussy out and she loved it. Her throat was still throbbing from when he fucked her in it earlier. She felt herself about to cum again.

A few more hard pounds against the wall made her squirt. She had heard about squirting but never did it until now. It was uncontrollable. Was she peeing? It felt so good at that point that she didn't even care as the fluids exploded from out of her body. She felt his dick inside her get slightly bigger followed by a warm sensation. He came. He came partly inside of her and finished on her thigh and stomach area. They were both exhausted.

A week went by and Cara woke up at 3 o'clock in the morning, drenched in sweat and shivering in ecstasy due to the exotic wet dream she just endured. This was not the first time she was having this dream. The curiosity of Dominique's sex game had gotten the best of her. The dreams have been getting stronger and more real for the past couple of nights. Her two year abstinence from sex had finally reached its peak and it was driving her insane. She was always able to avoid sex due to the high demand at her job, but since having dinner with Dominique, and that kiss. That kissed they shared would not get out her head. She got up out the bed and got in the shower. Just a few more hours to go before work and she had to calm herself down. She told herself that she would call Dominique to set up another date when she got off work.

Dominique was in the local barbershop, just getting out the chair of his favorite barber, when he received a call from Camille. He didn't recognize the number of course, however when he answered, she told him she got the number from Rebecca, and expressed how she would very much in need of his "services". She told him to meet her at the Victoria Secret fashion show in SoHo Manhattan. She agreed with the price he set for her, due to his presence at the show, it was higher than normal. Just like that he was booked. Dominique headed home, took a shower, got dressed, then jumped in his truck and began driving to the extravagant event. After and hour and a half commute, he finally arrived. He parked his car and walked past the long line up to the doorman. He gave his name to the man holding the clipboard. The doorman looked at his clipboard and quickly spotted his name. The doorman then proceeded to lift the velvet rope, allowing Dominique to go in. Dominique walked past exchanging head nods with the door man. When Dominique got in, he became star struck with the women inside. All of them were gorgeous. Every last one of them looked like the Victoria Secret Angels. The theme was Heaven's Palace. He headed to the bar to get a drink as he watched the models strut down the catwalk. He looked around to see if he could spot Camille, but she was nowhere in sight. He knew eventually she would make her presence known, so for the time being he was going to enjoy the scenery. On his second drink of Cîroc, an attractive woman sat next to him to order herself a drink. Her enticing fragrance grabbed a hold of his nose, causing him to deviate his attention towards her.

"May I get a Martini with 2 olives, please?", asked the fragrant lady.

"Sure, coming right up.", responded the bartender as he walked away.

"Let me guess, you need a drink before you

get on stage?", Dominique asked. The gorgeous beauty looked at him with a puzzled look on her face.

"Excuse me?".

"I said, smart thinking drinking alcohol to numb your stage fright.", he stated.

"There's no reason for me to get on stage. I am not a model.", she informed.

"What!", he exclaimed.

"Could of fooled me…. You should definitely think about doing so, because your beauty is top notch.", he charmed. The flattery seemed to win her over, because she began blushing.

"Well, thank you. That was nice of you. That may have been an idea about twenty years ago. I might have had a chance then. One thing I do know for sure is that you could be a model with that beautiful smile of yours.", she flirted.

"I would think about that but if I considered it, I would need an agent. Do you know of any?", he inquired.

"I'm qualified. Here, take my number.", she said as she hands him her business card. Dominique pulled out his business card that Ms. Rebecca got professionally done for him and handed it to her. She looked at the card and read aloud, "Mr. Dominique Vox". "Well Mr. Vox, it is a pleasure to meet you.", she said as she extended her hand to shake his.

"My name is Viveca Hines.".

"It's a pleasure to meet you as well Ms. Hines.", he said.

Viveca took another look at Dominique's business car and saw that it said, "Elite Comfort".

"So, Mr. Vox, what type of "comfort" do you provide?", she asked curiously.

Before Dominique could answer, his phone rang. It was Camille. She was asking for his location at the event. Dominique politely excused himself from his conversation with Viveca. Viveca placed his card in her clutch purse and told him they would speak another time soon. He continued his conversation with Camille and agreed to the meeting spot. Dominique found her located by the side of the stage. She embraced him with a careful hug. He remembered her from the dinner party but didn't realize how beautiful she was. She looked breathtaking in her stunning mini Gucci dress and slim waistline. She had a very nice physique.

"I'm glad you made it. I was beginning to think you wasn't coming.", she said.

"Why would you think that? Of course, I was coming.", he replied.

"I'm sorry for underestimating you. It's just that I'm so use to being disappointed, thanks to my husband.", she shared.

"We'll I'm not your husband.", Dominique responded slightly irritated.

"Your right and again, I apologize.", she said as she gazed at him one time over. She liked what she saw. She handed him an envelope stuffed with money. He placed it in his suit jacket inner pocket. Camille then grabbed his hand and guided him to a glam room in the back stage discreetly. Nobody noticed because they were all so caught up in the runway show. The room they escaped to had outfits in it that the models wore already. Once inside, Camille locked the door. She made sure it was securely locked. She then turned around and began kissing Dominique roughly. She was very feisty. She had wanted his cock since she saw him at the dinner party. She knew it was big and today she was going to confirm it. She started moving her hands slowly over his body until she reached his dick and began to grope it. She unzipped his pants and reached in it. She started to maneuver his dick through his boxers. He was already erect. She felt his precum through the boxers and it made her mouth water. She was dying to see it because the feeling was unbelievable. She dropped to her knees and took it out. Her eyes lit up like a Christmas tree.

"Oh baby! Fuck my mouth with that so I

can taste your cum.", she demanded. Camille had an unusual blowjob technique that was mind blowing and she wanted to share it with Dominique. She started by humming on his balls to get the cum in his sac boiling. Once she felt she pampered his balls enough, she maneuvered his dick in her mouth. It felt right at home. The warmth of Camille's mouth was unbelievable to him. She began slowly dredging his dick to the back of her throat. It created a feeling that made his toes curl. She then grabbed the both of his ass cheeks and pulled him towards her, giving him the indication to fuck her face. He took his cue and started poking her tonsils slowly while she swirled her tongue around his swollen dick. She got more turned on by listening to his increasingly excited breath and moans. He manhandled her into an upside down sixty nine position while still standing up. The sexual acrobatic move heightened her pleasure because she loved to be dominated. It made her feel like she was being taken. It was a secret fetish of hers that her husband knew nothing about. When Dominique couldn't withstand the pleasure any longer himself, he exploded in her mouth. She felt his hot cream splashing in the back of her throat. She consumed every drop. This brought her to her own orgasm. He put her back on her feet as she finished swallowing his cum as she wiped her mouth. He bent her over the makeup table and slightly choked her as he entered her pussy from behind. Stuffing her pussy with his horse sized dick made her cum unexpectedly again. He ignored her orgasm as he continued to fuck her with such urgency. Her ass bounced on his dick as he could see the white cream that came from inside her. She watched in the mirror as he was banging her hard from the back. Her pussy got hotter and more tingly as the pain from his thrust felt so good. He increased his hand on her throat, so her moaning was muffled. When he felt he was about to cum, he fucked her real hard and fast until he pulled out just in time for a huge gush of cum to splatter all over her back.

Completely drained and exhausted they both struggle to clean up, got dressed and sneaked out before curtain time of the event.

The next day Dominique jumped up out of
a deep sleep. He took a shower, got dressed
and decided to head over to Rebecca's
place next door. He hadn't seen her since
the dinner party, but she kept him booked
and busy. The dinner party seemed like
months ago. He was going to knock on her
door, but he decided against that thought.
He opted to see if it was open and to his
surprise, it was. He stepped inside, calling
out to Rebecca, but got no response. He
began walking through the house knowing
Rebecca was somewhere around. He looked
around the most obvious places, but still
didn't find her. He walked toward her
office. When he got in front of her office
door, he knocked and opened the door
simultaneously. To his surprise a man was
standing naked in front of Rebecca.

Rebecca was leaned back in her office chair enjoying the splendid vision of another well-hung stud. Dominique began to back out of the room as fast as he went in. He couldn't believe what he just saw. He didn't know how to receive it. Rebecca spotted him closing back the door and told him to give her a minute. He waited for her in the dining room, giving her some time to finish up what she was doing. She met him there moments later with a blissful smile on her face, greeting Dominique with an affectionate hug and sincere kiss on the cheek.

"God you smell good." she complemented.

"And so, do you, boss lady." he replied. He handed Rebecca an envelope of her half of the money from his recent "business transactions". She took the envelope, not opening it, not even taking the gaze off Dominique's handsome face and tossed it on the table.

"Glad I finally made it on your schedule." she stated. As he was about to bring her up to date on his recent endeavors, he was cut off by a male figure entering the dining room. He was a very handsome and well dressed in a tailored suit. He walked directly up to Dominique extending his hand to shake. Dominique reached his hand out to meet him halfway.

"It's an honor to meet you Mr. Vox, my name is Matrell Bryce. I heard a lot about you and let me tell you…. I am more than willing to help you with the load.", Matrell introduced himself.

"Nice to meet you Mr. Bryce." Dominique greeted. Dominique looked at Rebecca with a curious and confused stare, wondering what this stranger was talking about. Rebecca knew what the uncomfortable look was and so did her male guest, Mr. Bryce. The unfavorable expression on Dominique's face told Martrell that it was his cue to make an exit and leave them to discuss whatever it was that needed to be discussed. Martrell looked at his watch and seen that he was an hour ahead of schedule for his first date that Rebecca arranged for him. Still he decided to be someplace else until then.

"Well I'm gonna let y'all talk in peace. Rebecca, I'll call you later.", he said.

"Okay, you do that If you have any trouble finding that location, just give me a call.", she replied.

"Sure thing. Nice to finally meet you again, Mr. Vox" said Matrell as he extended his hand to Dominique once again. Dominique shook his hand with an attitude colder than an NY winter's day. Keeping his gaze at Rebecca.

"Yeah, okay!", responded Dominique. Matrell left like he didn't notice the cold shoulder he gave him. The sound of the front door opened and shut. Dominique quickly opened the conversation with the obvious.

"Can you please tell me what the hell is going on?", He demanded.

"Sure, why not. Your entitled to that. The

gentlemen that you just met, works for "Bedroom Thug.", she informed him.

"Bedroom Thug?", he asked as he repeated in an angry tone.

"Yes! A service I created for sexually deprived women.", she continued.

"I thought we was doing this. No other people. Excuse me if I'm confused here.", he responded.

"I'm sorry to disappoint you, Dominique, but I told you this was a lucrative business…So, I don't see how you would've thought I was going to get into this money-making business with just one hung stud. Two is not even enough. Matrell is one of many that I will be hiring. I have a few more coming over today and tomorrow. If they are qualified, then they will be representing my company.", she added.

Dominique sat back and listened to every word that came out her mouth carefully. He had to admit, he was kind of glad she was thinking like that. He was not trying to make a career out of this service. His plan was to make enough money and get out before he got swallowed into the lifestyle. He decided in that moment that he was going to keep his true intentions close to the belt. This would be the first time he wasn't completely honest with Rebecca and he didn't care.

"You right. You can't base your company on one person I can't please every woman. That's truly impossible. Do what you got to do. Who am I to get in the way?", he asked nonchalantly. Dominique began walking towards the front door but stopped by the sound of Rebecca calling his name.

"Dominique!", Rebecca called out. He turned around not saying a word.

 "Are you still on board?", she asked.

"Yeah, I'm on board.", he replied.

"Good! Because your still my main stallion. I need you to help me build this company from the ground up.", she encouraged. Dominique winked his eye at Rebecca and walked away with a slight smirk on his face. When he got to the door and opened it, there was a man standing there in the position of ringing the bell.

"I'm sorry to disturb you sir, but does a Rebecca reside here?", he asked.

"Yes, it is. She's expecting you. Please come in.", replied Dominique.

The young man stepped inside with a confident look on his face.

"She will be with you in a minute.", he continued. And just like that Dominique walked out of the house. A week later, Dominique received a call from Viveca, the female agent from the bar. He remembered the event and his conversation with Viveca so vividly. She wanted to meet up with him to discuss his business in more detail. They were interrupted the last time and she was eager to learn more about his trade. They agreed to meet on 34th street in Manhattan. She owned a loft out there. She gave him her address and they agreed on a time. Later that evening he arrived at the destination. He entered a large loft studio on the 15th floor of a luxury high rise. It was beautiful. This lady had to be a successful agent to afford this. The loft was very large and spacious. Lights, tripods, scenic backgrounds, reflecting umbrellas, and tight half naked men draped in open terry cloth robes and boxer briefs walked around the scene in front of him. It all slightly made Dominique feel uncomfortable. The last time he was surrounded by this many half-dressed guys was during an invasive search in prison. He promised himself that when he got out, he would never put himself in an environment that slightly resembled that, yet here he was. Dominique spotted a familiar female face from across the room. Standing next to a photographer was Viveca. She looked up, making eye contact with him. She gave him a warm smile and began to walk towards him. She wrapped her arms around him in a friendly embrace. He cautiously hugged her back. He was completely caught off guard and oblivious to what her intentions were. As they separated, her hands slid down his arms, stopping at his hand in hers. She looked him in the eyes and spoke.

"I'm glad you made it on such short notice. Was it hard to find?".

"No, not really. Please excuse me for being blunt, but…. I truly hope I'm not being rude, but...what exactly am I here for?", he questioned.

"Well the night we met at the Victoria Secret's fashion show, I was actually there for networking purposes. When I ran into you, I must admit that I was somewhat impressed. You carry yourself very well. You were very dapper, well-spoken and handsome. I thought to myself, I had to have you in my sheets. You have a lot of potential.", she added.

He listened intently as she spoke. She was kind of turning him on. The lust grew in his eyes. Viveca felt the sexual tension oozing off him. She broke the vibe with, "Are we on the same page here? I'm starting to think we aren't.".

Dominique's eyes grew big. Before he could respond, Viveca continued, "Have you ever heard of Bulge magazine?". Still not grasping her angle, he responded.

"I'm afraid I haven't."

"Well it's the number one male model magazine in the world. I am the head Editor and you are here because I see something in you. You could make us a lot of money. I would love for you to grace the pages for this upcoming issue. If the camera sees what I see, this could turn into a long lasting and lucrative relationship for the both of us.", she proposed. Normally he would of ran for the door. He wasn't one for a lot of exposure. However, listening to this complete stranger say she saw nothing, but positive attributes made him stay put. Intrigued by it all, he inquired, "What kind of money are we talking?".

"To be honest Mr. Vox, none of these men

you see here are getting paid for this shoot. They know and understand that the amount of exposure that they receive from gracing the pages of Bulge is payment enough. Having the right set of eyes fixed on your picture can and has led to some making a name for themselves and making possible millions. Some of these photos have led to profitable careers in modelling, acting, and the list goes on. I see you taking this opportunity to levels I have yet to see.", she attempted to entice him.

None of these opportunities ever crossed his mind. Acting and modeling was far from anything he ever thought of doing. Not once. Then again, he never imagined being an escort and he was flourishing in it. He decided then and there to take another chance. He was willing to step out of character and risk it all once again, but this time on a more positive note. Was it possible that this might set him up for life? He would never know unless he put himself out there.

"I don't know the first thing about modeling.", Dominique informed, feeling uneasy revealing his lack of confidence in anything.

"Don't worry about that. I'm sure you can take directions. I will coach you. You will be fine. Don't worry.", she encouraged.

"Okay...so you got me, huh? What do I have to do?".

"Glad you asked. Follow me.", Viveca said as she grabbed his hand and led him to the dressing room. The dressing room had different colors and designs of Calvin Klein underwear. She picked out the red, black and white boxer briefs. She thought the colors would fit his skin tone perfect. Viveca handed Dominique all three pairs of boxers with a cheerful look on her face. "That should do it. Any questions?", she asked.

"No, I'm just fine.", he replied.

"Well okay. I'll be outside if you need me.", she said before turning to leave.

"Yeah, sure.", he replied as he eyed the products.

Viveca left the dressing room so that Dominique can have some privacy to get dressed. A short while later, he emerged from the dressing room in some black boxer briefs with the confidence of a true model. When she seen his chiseled physique, she was in loss of words. His package was showing a desirable print. He had the body of a Greek God. Just what her magazine needed. She walked over to him with glee in her face. The magazine had hit the jackpot. Just as she thought. Now she just had to make the camera show it.

"Impressive. You look better than great!", she exclaimed.

"How are you feeling? Are your nervous?", she asked.

"No, surprisingly, I'm alright. I'm a little cold, but I'll manage.", he replied.

"Good attitude. I like that. Well look, follow me this way.", she said leading him over towards the area he would be taking the photos. Moments later he found himself in front of the camera, posing as if he been modeling for a living. The photographer was highly impressed. During the shoot he informed Viveca that Dominique was a natural. She thought so too. The photographer took 27 photos of Dominique before calling it a wrap. Dominique walked back to the dressing room to put his clothes back on. A couple minutes later, Viveca entered the room. She handed him a five-hundred-dollar check. He stared at it and then at her.

"What's this for? I thought the models don't get paid.", he inquired, puzzled at her gesture.

"I know it's not much, but the other men didn't get paid at all. I'm paying you personally for your time. I don't understand your business, but I kind of have an idea of what it entails. Hopefully you will take the opportunity to change that career. You are a nice young man, Dominique. I really mean

it when I say you have a lot of potential.",
she added.

"Thank you, Viveca. I kind of enjoyed
myself.", he replied. She thought he was
just being polite, she just hoped he took
advantage of this opportunity. He seemed
so much like a good dude. She sincerely
wanted him to succeed at this. As
Dominique is leaving the building of the
photoshoot, he received an unexpected
phone call from Cara. She wanted to see
him again. She invited him to come over to
her house so they could talk. He was
excited. The thought of her made him very
excited and horny. He agreed to the date.

Dominique arrived in front of Cara's address. He got out of the truck eagerly. Whether the night ended with sex or not, did not deter him from wanting to see her. He had to see her. Something about this girl made him nervous. He really liked her. He just wanted to spend time with her anyway he could. He rang her bell and began fixing his clothes as if he wasn't already dressed to impress. Moments later, Cara came to the door with a Victoria's Secret pink spandex outfit and fluffy bunny slippers. She wanted him to see her in her all-natural state and not dolled up. She had on no makeup and her hair fell loosely amongst her shoulders. He thought she looked extremely cute in her "house wear".

"Hey Dominique. How you been?", she greeted him with a smile.

"I'm doing fine. I can't complain.", he answered, returning the smile.

They both stared at each other dreamingly, until Cara finally remembered to invite him. Dominique stepped inside, walked up to her and kissed her on cheek as he walked past her. This sent a tingle between her legs that she had to contain. Behind his back, before she closed the front door, she closed her eyes and took in his scent. It was intoxicating. The combination of his cologne and kiss on her cheek made her pussy wet. "I'm sorry I must look a hot mess. I didn't have time to get dress", she stated with a weak laugh.

"You look fine. Matter of fact, you look great. I like it.", he replied.

"Are you hungry? Do you want something to eat? I can whip something up real quick if you like.", she offered.

"Nah, I'm fine. I ate not too long ago. Just happy you called and all.", he answered as he was admiring the setting of her apartment. She had a few scented candles burning, giving off a vanilla aroma. He also spotted a bucket with champagne sitting on ice, resting right next to the couch. "You have a nice place." he complimented.

"Thank you. I'm going to be remodeling in a few months...but anyway...enough about that. I know you don't want to hear me talk about that." she said.

"I don't mind you talking about anything. I love hearing your voice." he replied. Cara started blushing. She was so turned on by this man, it was unbelievable. She was anxious about his feelings for her though. She hoped the feelings was mutual.

"Have a seat. Make yourself at home, and I'll be right back." she stated as she headed to the kitchen to grab two flutes for the champagne. He sat down on the couch and watched her as she exited the living room. The site of her ass in the spandex, had his dick throbbing once again. Good thing he was sitting down because the cock was trying to stand up. He didn't want Cara to feel like he was some type of pervert. He tried to close his eyes and think of something else to calm it down. Cara returned to the living room with the two flutes for the champagne. She handed him a glass and sat down next to him with hers. She grabbed the remote of the coffee table and turned on her enormous T.V that she had hung on the wall. She tried to find an interesting movie. She settled for a romance flick. Dominique took the champagne out of the bucket to pour their drinks. After talking for more than an hour as the T.V played in the background, they both started to feel their drinks. The more Cara drank, the friskier she felt. On the surface she was cool and calm, but inside she was hornier than a mother fucker. As Dominique was speaking, Cara gave him a quick look over. Was it her imagination or was his dick hard? The bulge in his pants made her light headed. She refused to make the first move, no matter how soaked her panties got. Dominique on the other hand was caught up in her eyes. Damn she was sexy. She scooped her hair over to one side as she made herself more comfortable. He noticed her nipple ring print through her top. She wasn't wearing a bra. He felt his dick getting hard again. And he wasn't sure if his mind was playing tricks on him, but he could have sworn he seen her glance at his cock area. He leaned in and kissed her. She kissed him back right away, locking tongues and heavy breathing followed. She laid back on the couch with him on top of her. He began to lift up her top, exposing her pierced nipples as he was still tonguing her. He brings his face to her breast and starts to flicker his tongue across her nipples. Cara is moaning softly as his hot tongue continues on her breast. She reaches down to the dick print of his pants and started to caress it. She feels the size of his enormous cock and her pussy starts getting wetter. Things got real hot and heavy for twenty minutes of foreplay. Dominique got up and picked Cara up. She wrapped her legs around his waist. She feels his dick through her spandex, and she starts to grind against him while in the air. He grabbed her by her ass that always made him get an erection and thrust a couple of times against her pussy, so she could feel what was about to come once he got her out her spandex and drawers. The humping felt so good to Cara, but it also made her nervous, knowing she was abstinent for two years and his cock being so huge. For a quick second she thought to call the whole thing off, but then he kissed her again and sent that feeling of needing the sexual satisfaction. He carried Cara into her bedroom and laid her gently on the bed. He proceeded to help her remove the bottom of her spandex and her panties. He began kissing and nibbling on her inner thighs, sensually teasing her. Cara gently grabbed his head and moved it towards her pussy. He began softly sucking on her pussy lips. Satisfied with the taste he stuck his tongue in her pussy and began to tongue fuck her. He rotated between slow and fast as he sucked on her clit. Her body began to tremble. She came. He swallowed it up. He then eased himself up and removed his pants. His dick stood at attention with no hands. Seeing it in the flesh, had Cara horny again. He climbed back on the bed between her legs and opened her legs wider. He slowly inserted his dick into her. She tensed up. "Relax baby" he whispered in her ears. She tried to relax her legs a little, but his dick was so big. He gave a hard couple of thrust until he was fully inside her. Damn she was tight, he thought to himself. She let out a sexy groan and dug her nails into his back. Once he was all inside of her, he began to fuck her like he wanted to against his truck that day on their first date. He hammered down in her pussy, until she creamed with such a force that made her body shake the bed. The tip of his dick was rubbing hard against her cervix. She moaned loudly. He fucked her none stop with no mercy for 45 minutes. He finally came with such force inside her body. His hard body stiffened against her. He did not pull out. And she didn't want him to. She felt his hot cum shoot into her body. This made her have another orgasm. She wrapped her legs around him as his body collapsed on top of hers. He laid there for a couple of minutes before rolling off. She laid on his chest, listening to the beat of his heart. He began to gently caress her back. They talked for a while about various things. After an hour of chit chat, he laid her on her stomach, spread her legs and entered her again. He pounded her tight pussy until it became a non-issue to enter her walls. He fucked her from night until morning. They had sex for three days straight. He filled her pussy up with his semen each time. Not a drop was wasted. Even when she sucked his dick, whenever he was about to come, he would spread her legs open and bust off in her pussy. Same routine. Eat, shower and fuck. They fucked in every part of Cara's house. By the third day, sleep became their greatest desire. On the fourth day, Cara got up bright and early. She got in the shower, then got dressed for work. Her shift was usually at night, however they called her in for the morning shift. Dominique was still sound asleep. Her pussy was sore from all the fucking they done over the last couple of days. He surely met her expectation in the bedroom.

Better than her wet dreams she had about him. She loved that he treated her like a lady but fucked her like a whore. Thinking about it made her want to suck his dick before she went to work, but she knew if she started that, it would lead to other things and she wouldn't have made it in to work. So, she had to quietly finish getting ready for work. She softly kissed him on his forehead, wrote a note and then stuck it on the T.V screen on her way out. Shortly after, Dominique awoke from his sleep to take a piss and noticed Cara was not on her side of the bed. He first thought she was cooking something to eat, until he noticed the note on the T.V screen. He read it. Even though Dominique would rather spend more time with her, he understood. He respected how dutiful and ambitious she was. He thought that was one of her many sexy qualities. He decided to take a shower and eat something before leaving the house.

As one busy day drifted onto another, a whole year drifted by and the events of one year were lost in the dream of the next. Dominique and Cara were seeing each other for two years at this point. They rarely spent time together due to both of their busy schedules, however the time they did spend together was always made memorable. Their outrageous schedules had them preoccupied with their professional achievements, but no matter what they kept a close telephone relationship. Even though it wasn't much, they both treasure what they had. Since the relaunch of Bulge magazine, Dominique became a phenomenon. He gained 30 million followers on Instagram and 70 million on twitter. Most of his followers were women, of course. A month after his feature in the magazine, Viveca, from Bulge magazine thought it was a good business decision to release a Dominique Vox look book, which was a book full of sexy, explicit photos of him. The book was a success. It sold out everywhere in the first week. This led to a few movie deals on the table for small roles. Dominique was enjoying his success, basking in the limelight, hosting parties, doing underwear commercials, music videos, and still doing his escorting on the side. He became slightly addicted to sex. Dominique started his own escort business called "goodness on the go". Rebecca didn't know about it. Another thing he kept from her. He found and booked his own clients. He was doing that for a few months on the side. He still gave Rebecca a small cut, out of respect for bringing him into the business, but she had not booked him any clients for a while. Rebecca was too busy invested in Martrell. He still kept his meeting with the three regulars, Norah, Ariel and Camille. He loved the arrangements he had with them. Norah still buys him outlandish gifts and he gives her the anal pounding every other week. Camille still pays him to suck his dick every other day. She was always thirsty for his cum. She guzzled it like mouthwash and always ended with her swallowing. Ariel got the good hardcore. She couldn't get enough of his big black dick. One time he fucked her so hard she was walking funny for a week. shifted her uterus. Sometimes they got selfish with his time. Not wanting to share him with the other. They attempted to be more demanding by giving more and more money, but he let them know who was in charge. He was running things so much that he ended up having a three some with Ariel and Camille. He ate Ariel's pussy as he jackhammered Camille's throat with his dick until his cum spurted into the back of her throat. Then he made Ariel eat Camille's pussy as he fucked the shit out her from the back. When Ariel was about to cum, he removed his dick from her cunt, then made her ride Camille's face until she came in her mouth as he fucked the shit out of Camille's little pink colored pussy. He rough fucked them both and let them know only he was in charge. He treated them like the naughty little whores they were and they loved it. Some of his new clients only called him to have conversation, because they were feeling lonely and neglected by their husbands. Dominique built that trust with them to be able to open up like that. One thing that Dominique learned from Rebecca was that the escort business was a discreet business. His discreteness and professionalism, as well as charm, got him a list of rich, horny and unhappy housewives to please. Most of these women had professional careers and was more than willing to drop over $50k in cash on Dominiques lap, just to ride the horse with no strings and no risk of being exposed. Last month at an Armadale Vodka event, he met this fabulously wealthy, voluptuous and exotic Hungarian. She was a gorgeous well preserved 52-year-old woman. He couldn't believe it when she revealed her age to him. She looked like she could have been in her 30's. Before the event ended, she gave him her phone number and he handed her his business card. He left the event confident that she would become one of his clients. Before the week ended, she booked herself an appointment with him. She invited him to an all-expense paid trip to the South of France, where she was located. He went. Once settled into his hotel room, she had a chauffeured Rolls Royce limo sent to retrieve him. The limo pulled up to a gorgeous mansion and he got out. He went up and rang the bell. Moments later the door opened and there she was standing in a naughty French maid outfit with a smile on her face. Her breast was spilling out the top of the outfit. She had on eight-inch heels, that was honoring her legs, when she turned around and walked away. Dominique noticed she had on a red sequin and ruffle panties that hugged her curvy butt to perfection. He thought she was the dreamiest servant he has ever laid eyes on. The luxury weekend was pleasurable and gratifying. Plenty of kinkiness and fetishes being filled. Her guilty pleasure is lots of sex and she had a really high sex drive. The more she gets, the more she wanted and there was no satisfying that appetite. That's because she had no boundaries to what she didn't like her attitude was simply, "anything goes". Dominique like the fact that she had the need to please men. She wasn't selfish when it came to sex. She was obsessed with the idea and it made her feel guilty if her goal was not met.

Dominique slept the whole flight on the plane as he headed home. He was drained. Two days later he got a call from a movie director, telling him he got the role he auditioned for. He was so excited about the news that he thought it was a good enough reason to celebrate. There was only one special lady he wanted to share the good new with. That was Cara. He called up Cara and asked her to meet up with him. Cara could hear the cheerfulness in his voice over the phone. She agreed to the lunch date.

They agreed on a jazz spot on the lower East Side of Manhattan called, "Moldy Fig". He thought it was the perfect place because they be having live brilliant jazz players that plays proper, traditional jazz. He grew up on jazz music. He thought jazz music was the perfect music the air can carry. He was sitting down for twenty minutes embracing the beautiful sound of the saxophone being played by a local artist, when Cara came in strutting towards his table. He was in a trance, gazing at the way her hips swayed to the rhythm of the music. He hadn't seen her in weeks. Being in her presence now, he realized just how much he missed her. Dominique got out of his seat and Cara walked straight into his arms. He gave her a strong thorough hug followed by a plethora of kisses. Those kisses eased her anxiety. It made her feel warm, protected and cherished. She felt special. He made her feel this way anytime she was in his presence. They both sat down across from one another. Wasting no time, he bursts out, "I got the role!".

"Oh my God! That's so good baby, congratulations! I kind of knew you would.", she responded as she leaned across the table and planted a big wet kiss on his lips.

"I got news for you as well…", she continued. She waited to tell him in person. She wanted to see the expression on his face. Her news would be life changing for the both of them.

"I'm pregnant!", she exclaimed. As soon as she said it, a tear fell from her eye. Dominique stared blankly for a moment before a big smile spread across his face.

"Are you serious?", he asked excitedly with a quiver in his voice.

"Yep, very much so.", she added.

Dominique got up from his seat, and gently grabbed Cara by the hands, pulling her to her feet and hugged her tightly.

"Thanks for making me the proudest man in the world.", he whispered in her ear.

"I promise you, baby, I will be the best

father ever.", he continued.

"I know you will be baby.", Cara responded. She was so happy to hear him say the right things. She knew he was a good man, but she wasn't sure how well he was going to receive the news. She thought he may not have thought himself to be ready. She was excited about the pregnancy. The thought of becoming a mother was terrifying but she was up for the challenge. She was just ecstatic to have a partner that was up for the ride with her. Dominique announced in the jazz spot that he was going to be a father. The whole place applauded. A random person sent a bottle to their table. Of course, Cara wouldn't drink, so he drank for the both of them.

Months passed, Dominique and Cara were walking hand in hand on the red carpet at his movie premier. Paparazzi and fans alike were snapping photos of them and his co-stars. This night was a big deal. He looked dapper in an all cream-colored Tom Ford suit and Cara complimented his look with a matching cream-colored maternity Chanel dress. Their picture on the red carpet was captured on the front pages of all newspaper and of course, Bulge magazine.

When Rebecca returned from her vacation at St. Bart's a week later, the news of his relationship and pregnancy shattered her. She was furious. He never told her about that. She took it as a slap in the face. She was disgusted at the site of the "happy couple" on the cover. How could he betray her and start a relationship without her consent? Did that bitch of his know what he did for a living? She suspected something wasn't right by seeing less of him but was blindsided by the money she was receiving. In the beginning she didn't agree with his new-found fame, because she felt that he changed. At the same time, she was happy for him then because it was something, she felt she had helped create. Rebecca had a long list of men working under her escort service. Women were dazzled by the collective hotness when they visited the web-site, however, Dominique was her greatest creation. The real breadwinner above all her leading part in her business. Thanks to her one on one attention that she gave him, he achieved sex symbol status. And then he goes behind her back and pulls a stunt like this. She decided to call him to see where his mind was at. Deep down she hoped it was still on their mutual agreement. When she finally got in touch with him, he agreed to meet up at her house. He was glad that she had taken the initiative to meet with him. He knew he should have been called a meeting, but nevertheless the meeting was taking place now. As Dominique was driving to Rebecca's house, his intuition was telling him it was not a good idea. For some reason he felt the conversation would not be productive once he said what he had to say. He no longer wanted any dealings with that lifestyle. He no longer seen a future in it. It was as if he had a divine intervention to put his wild playboy days behind him. He changed his whole perspective thanks to Cara. She broke the mold, not even trying. She opened up his closed mind in ways he never could imagine. He had to consider his promising future as a model and acting, but most of all his responsibilities of becoming a father. The pregnancy was definitely a turning point in his life. The beginning was odd because escorting wasn't something he had planned for his life when he came home from prison, but things slowly progressed towards it. He generated enough money to say farewell to his sexcapades with lonely, rich and horny wives. As far as he was concerned, he served his purpose. All he wanted now was a normal life with Cara and the baby. It was the least he could do for the woman that he loves. Cara gave up her career to prepare for her future of being a stay at home mom. She was content with that.

Meanwhile Rebecca was oiling up her milky white skin, looking at herself in the mirror. She was loving how the lingerie hugged her curves just right. She had always been a confident cougar. She knew how to use her body to get what she wanted and what she usually wanted was good satisfying sex. Her plans for the night involved seducing Dominique back into her clutches. She didn't think that it was going to be hard, after all she easily seduced him before, and he helped her build her little empire. She had to remind him who was in charge.

Dominique pulled up on his old block and parked in front of his old house. It didn't look any different from the day he sold it.

Just looking at it brought back so many memories. Memories in which he was trying to escape. His mother and grandfather passed away while living in that house. The memories of those two weighed so heavy on his head, which was one of the main reasons he sold the property in the first place. He felt that if things didn't go right with Rebecca, then this would be the last of him seeing the neighborhood. Him and Cara had moved to LA a month after he got his role in the movie. They bought a nice beautiful house in Melrose. When he stepped inside, the familiar scenery lets him know what Rebecca was attempting to do, and he wanted no parts. Jazz music was playing in the background, candles was burning all over the place and a plethora of rose petals was on the floor leading to the living room. Dominique followed the rose petal path until he was in plain view of Rebecca, whom was laying seductively across her grand piano, mimicking her portrait on her wall. She smoothly slid down off the piano and began strutting confidently towards him. She was giving off a sexy glimpse of her pussy print peeking out her lingerie with every step she took. Her 8-inch fuck me pumps had her legs looking worshipful. He had to admit, he could not have been more pleased with the gesture, but he had to respectfully decline. He was there to give his resignation. He was there to let her know in person and out of respect that he was done. Rebecca, misleading Dominique's disposition correctly, assumes he is mesmerized by her beauty, but the truth was, he wasn't. She tried to kiss him, but he politely brushed her away by holding her back and turning his head, so her lips didn't touch his.

"Is everything alright?", she asked.

"Yeah, I'm fine.", he replied.

"You seem so tense, let me help you…."

"I just came to talk to you. Not all this.", he bluntly interrupted as he swerved her touch.

"We can talk after. Let momma take care of

you.", she said, as she tried to look seductively in his eyes. Dominique wasn't having it. He looked dead in her face as if he could kill, but still kept his composure.

"You're not my mother. My mother passed years ago!", he replied in a more serious tone. That was the first sign Rebecca picked up that whatever it was that bothered him, it had to be serious.

"You know what I meant, Dominique. Of course, I'm not your mother.", she stated.

"And I'm in no way trying to replace her.", she continued.

"You want to talk? Let's talk.", she stated as she turned away from him and started walking towards the couch. Dominique followed her not taking off his coat which was a clear indication that he didn't plan on being there too long. Rebecca sat down and gave Dominique her full attention.

"So, what's on your mind, sweetheart?", she asked. He wanted to choose his words wisely, because he wasn't up for any type of argument. His mind was made up and felt it unnecessary to go back and forth with her over this matter about his decision on his life. He wanted her to be happy for him and most of all, he wanted her to respect and understand when he makes a decision, he follows through. No one can divert him from that path.

"I know my worth.", he began.

"I mean, I been knew, but not sexually because I was so young when I went to prison. My mind is in another place and on another level. I regret selling my mind, soul and body so cheaply, however I know it was part of a process that helped me reevaluate who I am.".

"Stop talking in circles and get to the point. Speak. What's on your mind.", she interrupted him as she was getting annoyed and angry with him at this point.

"Okay, what I'm saying is, I'm done with this lifestyle. I want no parts of it anymore.", he stated clearly. There was a moment of tormented awkwardness in the air, as soon as the words left his mouth. Rebecca was stumped by it. She looked shocked and hurt. She started staring at him with a toxic look in her eyes.

"That's rubbish.", she said.

"Why the change of heart? Is it because of that bitch? What, she…".

"She's no bitch. That's my lady. Why you disrespecting her for?!", he interrupted.

"Why so defensive?", she questioned sarcastically.

"So, it must be her!", she added, as she got up from the couch and began pacing back and forth in the middle of the living room floor. Her "horns" were starting to show. She started getting loud and obnoxious.

"Everything is going smoothly. Why would you want to go fuck it up for some woman, you could have easily made a client?! What the fuck are you stupid??! Instead, you let this bitch reform your dumb ass. What, you think you're in love? AS IF? I know you. I know you don't love her, because you were still working our business until now!", she continued with a laugh. It wasn't just any laugh. It was some wicked witch type of laughter that you see in movies. He never saw or heard her speak like this before. He kept a calm and collected demeanor as Rebecca's rage grew.

"She's not like that is all I'm saying.", he continued.

"She doesn't deserve to be called out her name by anyone, especially by someone like you. You don't even know her to say anything about her…. Look, she's pregnant with my daughter. We're a family. Yes, I love her. I must be a role model for my daughter. I can't do that continuing to participate in this type of business. I told you from the beginning this was temporary.", he said as he tried to reason.

"I can call the BITCH whatever the hell I want. BITCH, BITCH, BITCH. I could care less about the bitch or her the demon seed she carries!!", she screamed.

"Dominique, you're a representative of a lucrative business that has great credentials and prominent potential to become something greater. Besides, YOU agreed to a long-term arrangement to see it reach its pinnacle and that's YOUR responsibility! I allowed you to have your little business on the side. Oh, you think I didn't know about your side hustle off MY idea? I knew honey and I allowed you to keep that. You don't respect me anymore…. you used me and got what you wanted and now you're done? At least you THINK you're done!" she raged on.

Dominique saw they were not going to find a common ground with her behavior at this point. "Rebecca, we had a general understanding from the beginning that this sex business was just a stepping stone for me. I capitalized and now it's time for me to move on. And for the record, it's my prerogative to do so. Out of the RESPECT, you claim I don't have for you, I came to tell you, face to face, that I was done. I could have done it by phone, but I'm here. I'm done. I wish your company much success. Oh, and one more thing…. please lose my number.", he said as he got up from the couch and walked out. You could cut the cold air with a knife. She was left standing in her hate. She felt humiliated that her seductive ploy didn't work. It damaged her armor to the point that her sinful thoughts were already set on something vindictive. She wanted revenge.

As Dominique was walking to his car, he thought about him and Rebecca's sexual encounters. He was going to miss them. He had to admit that he learned a lot from her. She made sex more than fun. Every time he was with her, it was like class was in session. Through her, he learned how to please women. He learned what women wanted and how to keep them wanting more. Thanks to all those one on one sessions, Dominique became a mega conglomerate in himself.

Three days later, Dominique and Cara took a romantic vacation to Venice. He heard it was a lover's paradise. All the stories he heard of the place, it was only right for him to see for himself if it lived up to its reputation. They checked into the Belmond hotel Cipriani. Cara had no idea that all their friends and family were flown in a day before. There was a big reason why he chose them to vacation in the most romantic place ever. The first night they stayed in the room. The second day they boarded a big beautiful yacht. To Cara's surprise, she came upon all her friends and family. She wasn't sure what was going on, but deep down, she had a clue. They greeted and mingled with everyone as the yacht sailed down Venice, Italy's Grande luxury resort and when it stopped, Dominique proposed to Cara with an 8-carat diamond ring. When she said yes, everyone present cheered with teary eyes. Her best friend April was extremely happy for her. Especially knowing what she went through with her ex, Kevin. The rest of the day was filled with more blissful excitement. The women were all admiring her engagement ring and rubbing, her forever growing baby bump. Cara became so drained and overwhelmed by all the excitement. Dominique closed the rest of the night up in the hotel room. They fell in love with Venice so much, that they decided the wedding would take place there.

Three months passed and Cara gave birth to a beautiful and healthy baby girl. She was 7 pounds 6 ounces. They named the baby Sophia. They never been happier in their life until they had her. Life was good. Cara finally had her baby to keep her company around the house while Dominique worked. He was doing a lot of that lately. His career had surpassed his own expectations. He tripled in fame and fortune. He built himself into a brand. From his first small role in the move to doing commercials, underwear modeling, TV show appearances and added four more movies under his belt. In those four movies, he had the starring role. His career and his life was in the greatest shape then it has ever been. He couldn't have asked for more, but for things to get even better. With him leaving the escort business left more time for him to be with Cara and the baby. Cara noticed he was around more and she didn't mind. She loved him and he loved her. The little things he did, like helping around the house, and keeping the baby while she got some rest, made her love him even more. She couldn't wait to be Mrs. Vox. As far as both of them was concerned, life was perfect.

One day when Dominique was coming home from a meeting with his agent discussing him being the face of a new cologne. He just finish finalizing the deal. He was in the process of going home to share his news with Cara, when two black S.U.V's pulled up on both sides of his car at the light on Hollywood Boulevard, and opened fire from both sides. He tried to duck into the passenger's seat as bullets riddled his car and body in broad daylight. The cars then sped off. People screamed and attempted to get out the way. Some captured the aftermath and it made its way through social media, all the way up to the famous, World Star. What seemed like forever, but was about 25 minutes later, an ambulance pulled up, performed CPR, and once they got a response, they took him to the hospital. He was still alive. Cara got the call an hour later about the incident and couldn't believe her ears. She was at the hospital in no time, sitting in the waiting area with their daughter, Sophia, in her arms. Dominique's agent and friends that he gained a closed bond with over time, showed up to show support. Everyone was astounded that something like this happened to him. Some was aware of his criminal past and being in prison, but his character and achievements outweighed that. After a few hours many of them left, however his agent stayed by Cara's side giving her words of encouragement. Also held baby Sophia, in order to give Cara's arms a break. Around 4' o'clock in the morning a doctor finally emerged from the operating room to speak to Cara.

"Mrs. Vox?", he asked. Cara looked up with pain in her eyes and stress in her face. Prepared to hear the worst but hoping for the best, she finally answered, "Yes, that would be me.", with a faint smile.

"Nice to meet you Mrs. Vox. I'm Doctor Sullivan. I'm the doctor that performed surgery on your husband in order to save his life. It was a critical but necessary surgery. Let me be the first to tell you that we won the fight, however it's just the beginning. He is critical, yet stable. Meaning he's still alive, but in a coma. It's too early to determine the amount of brain activity. We will have to wait and see. He's a very strong, Mrs. Vox, and I am very certain he will pull through.", he continued.

"Thank you doctor!" Cara said as she shook the doctor's hand while an ocean of tears flowed down her cheeks.

"Don't mention it. Trying to save lives is what we do, however talking to the patient's family is always the hardest part.", Dr Sullivan replied. Cara tears of anguish turned into tears of joy. She was relieved that Dominique didn't leave her alone. She was so overwhelmed because she didn't know what the future held once he came out of the coma. She held on to her faith. Dominique's agent stood up from his seat and shook the doctor's hand.

When the news spread about the attempted murder of Dominique's life, social media added insult to the injuries. Some people had nice things to say, but it was outweighed by bad ones. The rumors were ridiculous and rampant. People was saying some awful things, but the one thing that stuck out like a sore thumb and got under Cara's skin was when they called him a home wrecker and a male prostitute. She hoped that it wasn't true. All those times he wasn't home, she hoped it wasn't spent with other women. Cara thought to herself that out of all the things people could call someone, why that. She couldn't wait to get answers when and if he woke up. If the answer didn't feel right or add up, she was prepared to call the wedding off and leave with their daughter. Until then, she was going to support him until his health improved. Her routine from that day was going to the hospital to see him and taking care of their daughter.

Five months later in an early morning of July, that routine changed, when she got a call from the hospital about Dominique consciousness. Not only was he conscious, but he had use of 100% of brain activity. Cara was so happy that she rushed to the hospital in her pajamas. When she entered his room, two nurses just finished bathing him, which she never could get use to. She felt that was her duty as his future wife. She felt a little violated and jealous, however she knew it was their job, so she refrained from cussing them out. As she approached his bed with tears in her eyes and a smile on her face, his face lit up with joy. When he spoke, it seemed like it was a struggle. It was a low whisper, yet clear.

"Hey baby", he said.

"Hey baby!", Cara squealed. "I missed you so much.", she continued.

"I missed you too.", replied Dominique.

"I thought I lost you.", she said.

"I'm not going nowhere anytime soon. I haven't made you my wife yet.", he said. Cara smiled. It comforted her spirit to know him emerging out of something so dreadful yet remembering something so meaningful. She knew he loved her. There was nothing more important than to be his wife, but he had some explaining to do. This wasn't the time to address the issue. A couple of weeks went by, and finally he was discharged from the hospital. He was quietly thinking about his whole life on the ride home. He couldn't wait to be with his baby girl. He couldn't wait to see how big she gotten. As they were riding home, he noticed a black Mercedes Benz following behind Cara's car. He tensed up. Then he remembered that his agency told him that security was hired to watch over him and his family until everything was solved. When they first bought the idea to Cara, she was against it. She found it unnecessary, but due to them being so persistent with it, she finally agreed. She was glad she did at this point because she noticed every car that drove past them or besides them, Dominique's eyes were glued to it until it was a distance away. It pained her to see him in this condition. So unsure and not confident. It's like he had PTSD, and she understood.

When Rebecca got the news that Dominique was out of the hospital, she was at a Revlon makeup event. She was the host and enjoyed the attention. Every and anybody that was somebody was at this event. Even her top ten earners from her escort service. They were there networking, looking for prospects with money to give in exchange for a good time. Before the night ended, each and every last one of them left with a customer, so according to Rebecca, the night was a success.

As months came and past, Dominique got healthier and stronger. Cara never questioned him about the rumors. It was never a right time. He was walking, exercising and getting back to being physically fit. Viveca reached out to him, asking if she could get a cover story. At first, he was going to decline, but he remembered that it was her that was responsible for his legit success. If it wasn't for her placing him in her magazine, he would have still been out there selling sex. He felt the least he could do was agree to it. He agreed. Besides, Bulge magazine could be the platform he needed to showcase his comeback. It was a win-win situation for both of them and they both knew that. Viveca said when he was ready, she would be more than ready. He was excited about the idea. That's all he needed to hear for more motivation. Dominique worked hard to get his body physically fit to model and act again. The time came on that early spring. Viveca and her magazine team went to L.A. for five days, the first two days was all work and no play. They took photos of Dominique at different locations. Everybody thought the photos were amazing, so the last three days they partied like they were on a vacation. The last night got a little crazy when Dominique and Cara decided to leave the mansion party early. Soon as they got in the back seat of their awaiting Mercedes van, shots were fired. A couple of rounds hit the van before the driver sped off. Luckily the van was bullet proof. The second attempt on his life told him whoever wanted him dead had a strong desire for him to stop breathing, permanently.

Underworld Fortune Entertainment

Announces

<u>Upcoming Titles</u>

<u>Kiss the Ring Of the City</u>

<u>Gucci Girls</u>

<u>………Many More………</u>

You can get in Touch with Mark L Ford....

FB: facebook.com/UnderworldFortuneENT/

Email: underworldfortuneent@gmail.com